Cookbook

by Josh Langston

Copyright © 2019 Josh Langston
All rights reserved.

This is a work of fiction. Names, characters, places, and incidents either are the product of the author's imagination or are used fictitiously, and any resemblance to any actual persons, living or dead, is purely coincidental.

ISBN 13: 978-1732996458
ISBN 10: 1732996458

My favorite student! ♡ JV 8/19

Dedication

This tale is dedicated to my great friend, Mike Hammel. If there's a heaven, and I fervently hope there is, I suspect Mike looked over my shoulder from there while I wrote this book. I know he would have gotten a kick out of it.

Here's to you, Mike. We love ya, and we miss ya!

Contents

Acknowledgments
Chapter One 1
Chapter Two 17
Chapter Three 32
Chapter Four 48
Chapter Five 65
Chapter Six 82
Chapter Seven 98
Chapter Eight 115
Chapter Nine 133
Chapter Ten 151
Chapter Eleven 167
Chapter Twelve 183
About the Author 201
Bonus Chapter from *Oh, Bits!*

Acknowledgments

A grateful tip of the hat to the following who had the patience and fortitude to read through and comment on the original manuscript. These fine folks helped me produce a much more readable version of the story. It's unlikely I'd have finished as quickly as I did without their considerable input and valuable assistance.

Here's to: Annie Langston, John Langston, Don and Jan Wolf, Doug Tinsley, Carol Hammel, Doris Reidy, Pam Olinto, and Nancy James. Well done, everyone!

Chapter One

"The poets are the only interpreters of the gods."
—Socrates

Callie examined her face in the bathroom mirror. Despite the glare from the light, her left eye and cheek bore a familiar shadow, one which usually took two or three weeks to fade. She winced when Theo knocked on the door.

"Are you going to stay in there all night? I'm hungry," he called.

"I'll just be a minute." Callie touched the tiny gold pendant on a thin chain around her neck, and closed her eyes. She wished for long hair—long enough to cover her bruises, long enough to keep out the world. If she wished hard enough, maybe....

Theo pounded on the door. "You don't have to make such a big deal out of it, y'know. I didn't hit you that hard."

Callie pulled the door open and found Theo leaning against the frame. He reached for her, but she ducked away and hurried toward the kitchen. "I'm going to put some ice on it," she said over her shoulder.

Theo followed. "I wish you wouldn't make me do that," he said. He looked away when she pressed the compress to her cheek. "You don't appreciate half of what I do for you." He pulled a can of Budweiser from the refrigerator and tapped the top with his index finger before opening it. "This is the last one, you know."

"I'll get more tomorrow," Callie said. "On the way home from work."

"*Work?* Is that what you call it? Shelving books? Collecting nickels and dimes from geeks who can't keep track of what they borrow? That ain't work."

Callie forced herself to let the remarks slide. She'd heard them often enough, but she knew better than to ask him about his job. He'd been fired from the last one and hadn't shared any details about his search for another.

"You ought to plan ahead better." After chugging the beer, Theo walked to the front door and yanked his jacket from a hook. "I'll be back later."

"I thought you said you were hungry."

He checked his pockets for his lighter and keys. "I am. Hell, I'm starved, but I'm also sick of waiting."

Callie locked the door behind him. Alone, finally, she once again reached for the figure at her neck, a birthday gift from her great-aunt Enid. Callie had worn it non-stop since her twelfth birthday. Now, twice that age, she had rubbed the gold images of the olive leaf and the lightning bolt nearly smooth. Aunt Enid had told her they were symbols of the Greek goddess, Pallas Athena.

Callie closed her eyes, ready to make another wish, but then stopped. The wishes had never come true before, why should they start now?

~*~

"There's no cause for alarm," said attorney Gordon Parkhurst. "This firm has represented Enid Drummond for decades. Her taxes, accounts, and property have been maintained as carefully as if she managed them herself." He eased back in his leather upholstered chair. "Probably more so."

Theo and Callie sat near him in a walnut-paneled meeting room. Theo ground his teeth. "But nobody's heard from her in years."

The attorney smiled. "Certainly neither of you, anyway."

"She used to send my wife a birthday present every year. That stopped a long time ago. We're the only family she had."

"Actually, only your wife is a blood relation, Theodore," the attorney said. "You have no legal standing in this matter."

"Whatever." Theo shook off the distinction. "And I go by Theo, but it's *Mister* Flynt to you. So, when do we get to know what's in her will?"

The attorney shrugged. "That information will remain privileged until we have reason to believe Mrs. Drummond has passed away."

"Let's go," Callie said.

"She's a hundred years old, for cryin' out loud." Theo gave Callie a venomous glare. "And nobody's heard from her since you were a teenager!"

"Not exactly. I got a card from her for my twenty-first birthday."

Theo silenced her with a look that promised retribution.

Parkhurst remained nonplused. "Mrs. Drummond's extended absences are nothing new. She prefers to spend her time abroad. From our conversations in the past, I know she's particularly fond of Greece."

"So what? When was the last time she was gone more than two years?"

The attorney dismissed the thought with a wave. "Trips of two years or more aren't uncommon for her. She prefers living in Europe."

"Four years, then? Eight? Good God, she was in her nineties the last time she left!"

"She's a remarkable woman. I've no doubt she's quite well."

"I'll bet," Theo said with a snarl. "My guess is you people don't want to give up the service charges you skim from her account. I wanna know when you're going to hand over what rightfully belongs to us!" He jabbed himself in the chest with his thumb.

Callie put her hand on Theo's arm. "Maybe we should talk about this some other–"

He jerked his arm away. "At least give us the key to that old house of hers. We deserve that much. I wanna see some of what we're gonna get."

Parkhurst glanced at Callie. "I'm sorry, Mrs. Flynt, but I'm not authorized–"

Theo's nostrils flared. "Yeah, it figures." He stood up. "We're leaving."

Callie turned to the attorney, but Theo grabbed her shoulder and propelled her toward the exit. He stopped in the doorway and looked back at the white-haired lawyer. "As you people are so fond of saying: I'll see you in court!"

~*~

Theo dropped Callie off at the library then drove away as if chased by demons, his tires squealing. Callie shook her head. She had hoped they'd get a few more months out of those tires, but that wasn't likely the way Theo drove. If only he could control his stupid temper.

Resigned to another dull day, Callie walked up the steps to the library and made her way to the office. After dropping off her things she began shelving the returns, a job she actually enjoyed since it occasionally took her to subject areas she might never have looked into on her own.

As she worked her way through the library's collection of self-help books, she rounded a corner and collided with a familiar patron, Damian Dean.

"Gosh, I'm sorry," he said, backpedaling. "I had no idea–"

Callie shrugged it off. "My fault," she said. "I wasn't looking."

He seemed at a loss for words. "I– I didn't think you'd be in today." He paused and concentrated on her bruised cheek. "What happened to you?"

Callie turned slightly and palmed the bruise, hoping to appear casual rather than defensive. "It's nothing, really. Just a little bruise. You can see how clumsy I am." Her efforts to sell the lie with a laugh felt unconvincing. If only she hadn't run out of make-up the last time she had to hide Theo's handiwork.

"You're sure that's all it is?" he asked. He seemed genuinely concerned.

"It's sweet of you to ask," Callie said. "But really, I'm okay."

Damian smiled and gave her a little nod. "I'd hate to think anyone would try to…" He paused.

"Try to what?"

"Hurt you," he said with a slight blush.

"You don't need to worry about me," Callie said. She felt sure Damian had a crush on her, but she didn't want to encourage him. She may not have been in a happy marriage, but she was definitely not looking for someone to replace Theo. Still, the image of Damian Dean had popped into her head on more than one occasion.

"No one's trying to hurt me," she lied. "Honest."

He shrugged. "Whatever you say."

"I promise not to knock you down the next time we share an aisle."

Chuckling, he held up a book about self-defense. "I'm going to study up just in case. Can you check me out?"

"Sure." Callie had checked him out any number of times, and not all of them involved recording a due date for a book on loan. Damian stood an inch or two taller than Theo, but didn't have Theo's muscle or, thankfully, his attitude.

They walked side-by-side to the checkout counter.

"Are you seriously studying martial arts?" she asked.

"Sorta." His grin was infectious. "You never know when you might need to defend yourself." He paused again then looked straight into her eyes. "I'll let you know if the book's any good."

She tried to give him a stern look, but twisted her lips as she did it and decided the result must've looked completely dumb. "I'm really not in any danger."

He appeared to accept her words, picked up his book, and walked out of the building. Callie didn't notice that he'd left his wallet behind until sometime later as she assisted another patron at checkout. By then it was far too late to track him down. She stuck the wallet in her pocket with the intention of calling him when she got off work.

~*~

Theo wandered into the union hall still grousing about the asshole lawyer who refused to do anything about Callie's aunt. The woman had to be dead. Otherwise, why didn't she get in touch with anyone? No one had heard from her in forever. The more he thought about it, the madder he got.

He walked straight to the board where the union posted job openings. As usual, the specialties were all in demand–plumbers, electricians, masons, drywall mechanics–skills he didn't have or want. He didn't mind hard labor, but lately all those jobs went to guys who snuck over the border from South America, idiots who worked their asses off for peanuts and then mailed money back to wherever they came from. Total morons!

Compounding his indignity, he had to stand in line for a "No Jobs" ticket which he needed in order to collect his meager unemployment check. Callie's missing, rich-bitch aunt earned the blame for all of it. If only she'd just die!

People her age, and younger, dropped dead every day. Why couldn't she? With his luck, she'd outlive *him*.

~*~

Callie locked herself in the bathroom that evening, while Theo continued to fume. He'd gone outside to smoke, a rare concession she'd won after one of their many tiresome arguments. She leaned her head against the window, ear pressed to the glass, and waited. She heard banging as he took out his frustration by kicking the door. One of two things would happen next: he would come inside and start kicking *her*, or he would go to the bar and complain to his drinking buddies. She touched her necklace and held her breath.

More banging, then the wonderful sound of him leaving and then gunning the car engine. She watched the taillights disappear down the narrow street and waited a few minutes to be sure he didn't come back. He would be gone for hours, maybe all night. She didn't unlock the bathroom door, though. Not yet.

Quietly, as if she were a burglar, she opened the cabinet under the sink. Reaching far toward the back, she withdrew a box of sanitary pads. Craning to hear any noise from outside, she eased the box open and reached under the pads, a place where Theo would never consider looking.

The cold metal key—her entrance to aunt Enid's shuttered estate—remained right where she'd left it.

~*~

The usual crowd occupied Toni's Bar and Grill, and for Theo Flynt, the place felt like home. He liked the mixed aroma of tobacco, beer, and sweat that permeated the place. Only his kind of people went there—tough, self-reliant people—the kind who appreciated the wrestling photos on the walls. He admired them, though he often complained Toni had skimped on pictures of the female grapplers. Oh, how he'd love to go a round or two with one of the gorgeous Ring Divas who made the Monday night matches so much fun to watch.

He couldn't afford cable, so he had no choice but to watch on the big screen at Toni's. Not that he minded; it got him out of the house and away from his clingy wife. If not for the inheritance she would soon receive, he would have left her long ago. Best of all, it gave him more time with his pals.

"Yo, Flynt," called the tavern's owner, a woman taller than most of her patrons, an illusion she maintained by standing on a long platform behind the ancient wooden bar. The platform gave her a slight vertical advantage over her clientele. "The usual?" she asked.

"Yeah," Theo said as he dropped into an open space in a wooden booth occupied by two others. He preferred to have a view of the front entrance, and his friends humored him by leaving the spot open.

"You're runnin' late, Flynt," said the larger of the two, nodding at a TV screen over the bar. "Show's about to start."

"Who's on tonight?"

"Does it matter?" asked the third occupant of the booth. "They're alla same to me." He went by the nickname of 'Salty' owing to a summer he once worked on a fishing boat somewhere in Canada.

"Shuddup and drink, Salt. All yer taste is in yer mouth."

"What he said," added Flynt as he bumped fists with the big man sitting across from him. "I didn't miss anything, did I?"

Big Lou shook his head. "Just some music and the usual commercial shit." Of the three, Big Lou was the intellectual. He often used words Theo didn't understand, though Theo would never admit it. He knew he had as much on the ball as Big Lou, he just lacked the other's education. Theo didn't envy him; education was over-rated.

"Aw, shit," groused Salty. "Heavy weights. Geezus friggin' Christ. Why they gotta trot them cows out agin?"

Rather than respond, Theo watched as Wanda, Toni's only waitress, delivered his beer. She looked about as old as his wife's aunt. "You want anything to eat?" she asked.

"Nah." He dug his hand into a shallow bowl of peanuts on the table. "These'll do." He popped a few into his mouth and chewed, then focused on Big Lou. "You know anything about inheritance?"

"Maybe," Lou said, a note of boredom in his voice. "Is this about your wife's old aunt again?"

"Yeah."

"Be patient. The old biddy'll croak one of these days, and everything will be cool." He paused to belch. "You'll be buyin' our beer for as long as we live."

"What if there's no proof she's dead?"

Lou yawned. "I think there's some kinda deal where a person can be declared dead if they've been missing long enough."

"How long?"

"Do I look like an ambulance chaser? How the fuck would I know?" He drained his beer and signaled Wanda to bring him another.

"We talked to the old bat's lawyer today," Theo said.

"He's some piece of work. Says I'm not entitled to anything even though I'm Callie's husband. How's that for shit?"

"You'll be entitled to half once she gets it," Lou opined. "That's the law, unless she made you sign some kinda prenup."

"Some kinda *what?*" Theo squinted at him. "Bitch can't make me do nothin'."

"A prenup is a thing you sign before you get married. It says what you can claim in a divorce."

"I didn't sign anything except the marriage certificate, and now I'm wondering what in hell made me do that."

"Love," said Salty. "You fell in love."

"Fuck you, Salty. Go back to Nova Scrotum." Theo washed another handful of peanuts down with beer. It seemed a little flat.

Lou went on, "If Callie is the old lady's only living relative, she should get everything. Unless..." He paused as if he'd lost track of where he was going.

Theo tapped him lightly on the arm. "Go on."

"Oh. Yeah. I was just thinkin'. If the old gal wanted everything to go to charity, you'd both be screwed. That'd suck for sure."

"No shit." The possibility renewed Theo's anger at the woman he'd met but once, long ago.

Big Lou emptied the peanut dish into his mouth and chewed. "That don't seem likely, though. And besides, there's nothing you can do now 'cept wait. I'd wager the worst you'll get is half."

Theo blinked. "The worst? You mean I could get *more* than half?"

"Sure. All Callie has to do is collect the inheritance and then die, leaving it all to you. Does she have a will?"

"Nah. I'd know if she did."

"Huh. If I was you," Lou said, "I'd make damn sure I was the only beneficiary."

"Guys!" groused Salty. "Take a breath, will ya? The heifers are done, and the real Divas are about to git rollin'."

~*~

If not for a recently opened bus route, Callie might never have been able to visit Enid's dark, Victorian estate in the swanky suburban area of Atlanta called Buckhead. She entered through a side door and went straight to the parlor.

Standing near a marble counter built into a wall, Callie ran her fingers just under the overhanging edge, feeling for the outline of a tiny switch plate embedded in the supporting woodwork. It responded to her touch, and a section of paneling across the room slid sideways into the adjoining wall. Callie hurried through the opening. The paneling whispered shut behind her as she climbed a narrow stairway, the only route to a small room on the top floor.

"This is my private place," Enid had once told her. "You and I are the only ones who know it even exists."

Lined with shelves, the room's only furnishings consisted of a Tiffany-style reading lamp, an overstuffed leather armchair, and a roll-top desk. The shelves provided space for a host of treasures Enid had collected around the world.

Over the years, Callie had investigated them all, along with Enid's little notebooks—one for each of the objects on the shelves. Enid gave her access to everything except a single locked cabinet above the desk.

Callie sank into the armchair, grateful she'd worn

shorts and a sleeveless blouse; she loved the feel of cool leather on her bare skin. The chair also gave her a sense of arms-around protection. While hidden away in Enid's secret loft, Theo could never find her.

She gazed at the locked cabinet. Everything in the room was valuable—Enid wasted no time on the mundane—so whatever she stored there must be extra-special, or possibly even dangerous. Callie stood and approached the cabinet. She put her hands on the smooth wood and examined it as she had so many times before. No knobs or hinges marred the soft gloss of the surface, and even if she had a key, she couldn't find a place to put it.

Enid once told her she would be able to open it when the time was right. Callie couldn't help but wonder why she felt the need to be so cryptic.

A clock beside the cabinet signaled the hour with a muted chime. The sound drew Callie's gaze. She'd never liked the ornate timepiece. Heavily decorated in gold and ivory, it seemed too mechanical—out of place among the ceremonial masks, statuary, and ceramics.

Callie had read Enid's notes on each item in the collection, from the statue of the Sumatran fertility goddess to Thor's hammered-gold drinking cup, and from the devil-summoning drum of ancient Senegal to the horn-handled, spirit-killing dagger of some long-dead Lapland king. Though charming, Enid proved in every case they were all just superstitious nonsense.

Had Enid left a treatise on the clock, too? Callie couldn't remember seeing one. Staring at the gaudy decorations on the clock, she suddenly realized why they looked so familiar. The grape leaf and lightning bolt motif were identical to the charm on her necklace. She looked more closely and discovered a smooth spot, as if a piece of the decoration had been pried off.

Callie fingered her necklace. Could this be it? Would Enid have defaced one of her treasures for the benefit of a child? It didn't seem likely, but still....

She pulled the delicate gold chain over her head and held the little charm next to the clock. The outlines were identical. Holding her breath, she pressed the charm into the matching cavity, and the locked cabinet below clicked open.

Trembling with excitement, Callie peeked into the open cabinet. Inside she found a wooden tray filled with tiny porcelain jars, and another of Enid's notebooks.

~*~

Damian Dean sat at his kitchen table trying to concentrate on the self-defense book he'd checked out of the library. Success eluded him.

His mind kept returning to the young librarian, "Callie" according to her name tag. He didn't know her last name, but he knew something more important. Someone had hurt her, and it had happened more than once.

Damian had no illusions of being a hero. He had no faith in his ability to render justice, on his own, to whomever had left the bruise on Callie's pretty face. But he remained angry about it and determined to do *something*. He just didn't know what.

It made no sense for Callie to say she wasn't in danger; her demeanor reflected her fear every time she came to work bruised. Her efforts to hide the damage with makeup seemed a little too obvious, as if she wanted to call attention to her wounds rather than camouflage them.

"Then again," Damian cautioned himself, "you could be letting your fascination with the library clerk over-ride your better judgment. It's not like your track record with the fair sex is all that hot."

He looked at another title he'd previously checked out of the self-help section of the library. **Build Yourself From the Inside Out**, the title proudly proclaimed.

He hoped the self-defense book had better suggestions. His insides hadn't changed much since he read either book.

~*~

Aristotle Spanos strolled into his suite at the hideously misnamed Alexandrian Hotel in downtown Atlanta. While the owners had spent a great deal of time and money on the place, they'd focused on Roman artwork and artifacts rather than anything which actually commemorated the world-conquering hero of ancient Greece.

Idiots! They wouldn't last a day in my *employ.*

If Spanos hadn't just been released from prison, he might have objected more strenuously, but regaining his independence and returning to his lifelong quest took precedence over such lesser issues. He would have plenty of time to decide if firing the incompetent who'd booked him into the Alexandrian was enough. Punishment would certainly be an option.

Spanos held punishment in high regard, provided, of course, he wasn't the one suffering. Ensuring his buffer from that required a great deal of money—mostly in the form of billable hours to attorneys and untraceable payoffs to bureaucrats. It had been worth it, however, as evidenced by his recent incarceration. The five years he spent in a minimum security facility could have been much, much worse. Having received time off for "good behavior" made his release even more delicious.

The gods surely favored him, since his prosecutions had all been for white collar crimes. He hadn't been connected with anything worse. It still made him smile. They had no idea what real horrors he'd instigated. He aimed to keep it that way, and if he found the rest of the treasure he'd been searching for so diligently, that would be assured.

Shakespeare had it right. "What fools these mortals be."

Chapter Two

"India has two million gods and worships them all. All other countries are paupers; India is the only millionaire."
—Mark Twain

Callie took pains not to upset anything as she eased the delicate wooden rack out of the cabinet and set it on the pull-down surface of the roll top desk, then reached back in for the notebook. While most of Enid's notebooks were of fairly common origin, this one couldn't have been more different.

The cover had been crafted from exquisitely soft leather, and the thick pages felt as if they had been made by hand. Thick, and slightly textured, they would have provided the perfect background for Enid's beautiful handwriting, except that the words written there were obviously scribed by someone else.

Callie adjusted the lamp in order to read the labels on the miniature porcelain jars, each of which had a matching pottery stopper wired in place. She lifted the first of the tiny containers and squinted at the lettering, but it made no sense.

Zeus's Cookbook

Ἀχελωίς

Knowing her aunt's affection for all things Hellenic, she guessed the word had been written in Greek.

Swell.

"Thanks, Aunt Enid. I studied the classics, but I didn't have to be fluent in Greek to do it. How am I supposed to know what all this is for?"

Thumbing through the notebook, Callie came upon a sticky note which read:

Calliope– The set is not complete. I have Ήβη, *among others. I'll explain later, when we meet. I just don't know when that will be. In the meantime,* καλή όρεξη!   *Love, Aunt E.*

"Well, that explains things!" Callie squinted at the row of miniscule containers with their odd-looking labels and shook her head in frustration. "What in the world am I supposed to do with them?"

One thing she did know–Theo wouldn't be seeing the curious collection, much less hearing about it. Callie pocketed the sticky note along with the little container she'd first removed from the rack then replaced everything in the cabinet. When she pushed the door shut it responded with a satisfying click.

"Time to go home and feed Theo," she said to the empty room, but she was far more interested in getting back to the library where she could use one of the computers there to look up the Greek words her aunt had used to tease her.

The more she thought about the riddle she'd been left

with, the more she appreciated her aunt's perception. She knew Callie wouldn't rest until she'd figured it out. She also knew Theo lacked the curiosity and the intellectual capacity to do it himself.

Thoughts of Theo depressed her. She'd often considered getting a divorce and moving to Europe in search of Enid. Her husband, however, had already declared they would be together forever, a prospect she grew to despise more every day.

~*~

Big Lou's question simmered in Theo's brain as he drove home. Watching the wrestling match had provided some distraction, but the possibility Callie could have a will—that she might have left instructions to screw him out of what he was lawfully entitled to—made him grip the steering harder and harder. He barely noticed when he smashed into and then parked on top of their garbage can.

When I get the old bitch's money I can buy a hundred trash cans. A thousand. Who the hell cares?

His anger grew when he discovered the locked door to their apartment.

"Damn it, Callie!" he yelled. "Open the friggin' door."

From somewhere inside he heard, "I'm coming."

He toed the door with his foot, hard. "Hurry the hell up, will ya? I'm tired of standin' out here."

"Okay, okay," she said, her voice muffled.

He heard the latch and chain, followed by the deadbolt and pushed the door open as soon as he could. "What the hell? You lockin' me outta my own house now?"

She backed away as he advanced toward her. "I– I

always lock up when you're gone."

He sneered at her. "Why? What're you 'fraid of?" He slowed his speech so the words wouldn't sound slurred. He knew he wasn't drunk; he sure as hell didn't want to sound like it and give her something else to bitch about.

"I'm sorry," she mumbled. "I didn't know when you'd be back. This isn't the greatest neighborhood, y'know."

"Oh, so now it's the neighborhood. I can't provide a decent place to live, that it? Geez. Wha' the hell d'you expect?"

"Not much anymore," she murmured, still backing away. "And yeah, I get scared sometimes. I've seen gang bangers wandering around. I've heard shots, too."

"How come I've never heard 'em?"

"'Cause you're usually not here at night."

"What the hell's that s'posed to mean?" he snapped, giving her a quick backhand.

She stumbled away, holding her cheek. "It's nothing. Nothing at all. I get it. You need some time with your friends. I'm okay with that. Really."

"Bullshit. You hate my friends."

She stopped backing up when she ran into a wall. "What's the matter? Why are you so angry?"

"Maybe 'cause I don' like bein' cut outta your will."

Callie's eyebrows drew together in a tight line. Her lip quivered. "What're you talking about? What will?"

"*Your* will!" he said, his voice rising. "You cut me out!"

As he drew back his arm to deliver another slap, one she richly deserved, she slipped out of reach and shifted into the area they called their "living room." She stayed out of arm's reach by keeping a sofa they'd obtained from a church-sponsored thrift store between them. If he moved one way, she moved the other. So stupid, and so tiring. He didn't feel like running after anyone, even someone who'd betrayed him as Callie had.

"I don't understand," she whined. "I don't have a will."

"Big Lou said–"

"Who's Big Lou? And what does he know about me?"

"He's a friend. Smart. Real smart. He…" Theo continued winding down; fatigue sapped his rage. He didn't know why, exactly. He just felt… tired. So friggin' tired.

"This is dumb," Callie said. "We're arguing over something doesn't exist. You're mad at me for doing something I haven't done. I promise. I do *not* have a will."

Theo shook his head to clear it, but that only made the room unsteady. Keeping his balance required an act of will. He grabbed an arm of the sofa for support.

"Why don't you lie down on the couch," Callie said. "Stretch out. Get a load off. Relax."

He dropped onto the middle cushion and slumped sideways. She helped him lie down. He had to admit, it felt good. Damned good. He might've had a little too much to drink. Wasn't his fault. The guys were buyin' beer by the pitcher. He vaguely recalled buying a couple himself when his cash ran out. He remembered that distinctly. The ugly old broad who worked for Toni had given him a look that reminded him of his teen years when he came home a bit tipsy, and his mother acted like he'd caught some dread disease. What the hell was the waitress's name? *Wilma? Wanda? Something like that.*

"We'll talk in the morning," Callie said.

"Whatever," he muttered as the lights went out.

~*~

Callie loved being at the library early; she had the place to herself. She often volunteered to open since it got her out of the house and away from Theo before he got too horny, or abusive.

She strolled over to the bank of computers made available to the public and brought them to life, one at a time. After a brief wait, she sat behind a console near the back wall, out of sight of early patrons.

As the log in screen appeared, she thought back to the previous night. Theo had come home blasted, as usual, but he'd found a new focus for his anger. *A will?* The only will they'd ever talked about was her aunt Enid's. Why would he think she had one, too?

It was Big Lou, whoever he was. He put that crazy notion in Theo's head and left her to deal with it.

A will probably wouldn't be a bad idea, she thought, especially if she ever did inherit something from Enid. However, the concept of making Theo a rich man by leaving everything to him made her queasy. The world didn't deserve a jerk like Theo; making him rich would only create a bigger, meaner, more entitled jerk.

No. That wouldn't do. *Ever.* If she had the chance, she'd leave everything to an animal shelter or an organization that helped battered women. If all else failed, she'd leave it to a clown college. That would really drive Theo over the edge.

She liked that idea—a lot. All she had to do was put some money aside, enough to pay the attorney's fees for a simple will. It couldn't cost that much. Unfortunately, Theo made her turn over her paycheck, as paltry as it was, to him.

He even went over the grocery receipts she brought home. She never could understand that. Still, she managed to score a little spending money by buying things she could later return for cash. Theo hadn't caught her at it yet, but she had no illusions about how he'd react if he did. She palmed her bruised cheek and tried to ignore her reflection in the nearly blank computer screen.

Knowing she had to push such thoughts out of her mind, Callie focused on the task at hand. She logged on to the PC and called up the Internet. From her pocket she pulled the tiny ceramic vial she'd taken from Enid's house and set it beside the monitor.

Ἀχελωίς

The label taunted her. How was she supposed to type in letters for a language she didn't know? It looked like Greek, but then, just about anything that wasn't English, Asian or a hieroglyphic fell into that category. There had to be a translation program somewhere, but she'd never needed or used one before.

After a few false starts, she located an application that she thought might work. It allowed her to enter a word or phrase in any of two dozen languages. She could then choose a second language into which the text she entered would be translated. Best of all, it didn't require her to buy or subscribe to anything. Theo would never allow her to have a credit card.

She selected Greek for her input language and matched the letters on the vial with the letters in a chart of the Greek alphabet. Many of the capital letters she recognized from the names of college fraternities and sororities, not that she'd ever joined one. Night school and a day job didn't leave the time, energy, or money required for that.

After working her way through the label, she selected

English for the output language and pressed ENTER.

In seconds, a word appeared: *Achelois*.

This just keeps getting stranger and stranger.

Callie stared at the word, trying to decide if she could even pronounce it. Had the program made a mistake? What in the world was an Achelois?

"You can look it up, y'know."

Startled, Callie turned in her chair and stared into the smiling face of Damian Dent.

"I'm sorry if I surprised you," he said. "I didn't mean to."

She felt herself blush, then felt foolish for doing so. "It's– It's okay. I just got caught up in what I was doing. I'm afraid I'm not much of a computer geek."

"Me either," Damian said, "but I know a couple tricks. May I help you?"

She responded with a little laugh. "I think that's my job."

"But maybe not *this* morning," he said as he seated himself in a rolling chair next to hers. He reached toward her keyboard and paused. "May I?"

"Sure." Callie rolled to the side to give him some room.

Damian highlighted "Achelois" and copied it into keyboard memory then opened a new search window, pasted the text into a browser, and pushed ENTER.

Almost instantly, the computer responded with:

Achelois (From ancient Greek: Ἀχελωίς, Ἀkhelōís means "she who washes away pain") was a name attributed to several figures in Greek mythology. **Achelois**, a minor Greek moon goddess.

"How'd you do that?" she asked.

He gave her the briefest of tutorials and suggested she practice her new-found skills, which she did.

"This is amazing," she said, pleased to have mastered the maneuver easily. "I wish it were all this simple."

"Me, too," he said, squinting as he looked at her cheek.

She resisted the impulse to cover the bruise with her hand. "What is it?"

"Uh… Nothing," he said. "Is there anything else I can do for you?"

"No," she stammered. "This is great. You've been a huge help." She conjured up a smile and looked from him back to the computer screen. "Now all I need to do is figure out what all this means."

"You will. And listen, I'm in here a lot. So if you need me, just call on me." He stressed the word "need" but matched her smile with his own. "I really mean that."

"You've been a huge help," she said. "But I think I can manage on my own now."

She watched him wander away without looking back and instantly regretted not trying to get to know him better. And why not? If Theo could have friends, why couldn't she? Then reality set in. Theo. He'd make sure anyone who wanted to befriend her wouldn't stick around long. He wouldn't allow her to have a pet, much less another human with whom she could associate.

And he thinks I'm clingy. Resigned to her fate, Callie took another look at the computer screen.

Achelois—the ancient Greek name for a minor moon goddess.

Huh?

She used the same browser Damian had called up to get some information about the goddess. What she learned didn't make much more sense than what she already had. It did, however, give her another idea.

~*~

Theo congratulated himself on showing so much restraint. The moron at the union hall deserved a lot more than he got, a beat down at the very least.

All Theo did was ask why they hadn't posted any good jobs lately. The response had been a snarky, "Maybe if you came in before noon, you'd find something."

What a pissy thing to say to someone who only wants to work. Theo wanted to shove the job board down the man's throat, or maybe up, from the other end. Either way, Theo would have been satisfied. Instead, he merely flipped him off and walked out the door.

Fortunately, a short walk brought him to Toni's place. The car was almost as low on gas as he was on cash. He hoped Toni would let him coast for a while. She knew he'd be good for it.

Toni, however, didn't come in until later in the day, and as Theo settled onto a barstool, he found himself facing Wanda, the waitress. She looked a lot taller standing behind the bar, but the lighting didn't do her any favors. She still appeared to be in her eighties.

"Gimme a tall draft," Theo said.

She eyed him suspiciously. "You gonna be able to pay for it?"

"Yeah, sure. In a day or two. Toni lets me run a tab."

"Toni isn't here."

"I noticed."

"You're awful early, aren't ya?"

After his run-in at the union hall, the last thing he wanted was another wise ass telling him what to do. "You're awful ugly, aren't ya?"

"Is that the way you sweet talk Toni?"

"Just gimme a goddam beer," Theo said. "I don't need any grief."

"Do you see the word 'charity' posted anywhere in here?" She went on before he could respond. "Come back when you can pay, like everyone else."

"Listen–"

"No, *you* listen. I've gotta work for my money, same as you. You want something for nothing, go get a tin cup and beg for it. Now get outta here. You're taking up space and wasting my time."

"You'll regret that," Theo said as he slid off the barstool.

Wanda reached down and pulled a baseball bat from a shelf beneath the bar. "Yeah? When? Now, or later, after you get outta the hospital?" She laughed. "You'll have to pay them, too, ya know. Brain surgery ain't cheap, but then, you don't have much to work with."

If she hadn't looked so damned confident, so ready to swing the bat at him, Theo would have climbed over the bar and shown her who had brains. Instead, he once again exercised restraint and sauntered toward the door.

Two Latinos stood in the open entrance, blocking his path.

They were prob'ly the ones who got my jobs!

Theo lowered his shoulder, football-style, and aimed for the narrow space between them. Much to his surprise they didn't separate to let him pass. Instead, they closed the gap.

Theo didn't slow down. *If that's the way they wanna play, fine.* He drew back his fist.

Sitting at a nearby table was a third Latino Theo hadn't noticed. He stuck out his leg, and Theo tripped over it. One of the two at the door attempted to catch him before he hit the floor, but Theo twisted away from him and kicked his companion in the shin.

The trio wasted no time treating Theo to a flurry of kicks from all sides.

Whimpering in pain, Theo curled as tightly as he could while the beating continued.

Eventually, Wanda's voice broke through the melee, and the kicking stopped. Theo hurt everywhere, and despite his attempts to cover his head with his arms and hands, more than one blow had breached his defenses. Blood dripped from his nose and face, pooling on the floor.

"Get outta here, Flynt," Wanda grumbled. "Now I've gotta clean up another mess you've left behind."

"Screw that," he muttered, probing his mouth with an index finger to check for loose teeth. "Call the cops!"

"Why? 'Cause you attacked three paying customers, and they fought back?" She waggled the baseball bat at him. "Go pound sand, slacker."

Too sore and frustrated to respond, Theo struggled to his feet and shuffled outside. It would be a long walk home.

~*~

Damian Dean felt mixed emotions as he sought refuge in the self-help section of the library. Having thoroughly enjoyed showing the cute librarian a digital shortcut, he'd hoped she'd lean on him further. Those thoughts vanished when he saw the new bruise on her face.

Though he managed to clamp down his immediate reaction, he still seethed with outrage over the fact someone had hurt her.

He knew she was married; the cheap gold band on her left hand made that clear. No wife of his, assuming he had one someday, would have to settle for a cut-rate, discount store wedding ring. A great one didn't mean great love, but a cheap one and bruises told an all too common story.

Based on her modest, faded wardrobe, Damian figured she lacked the funds to escape, assuming she wanted to. From what he'd read and heard, many women found ways to excuse their abusive husbands for the harsh treatment they doled out. Others, however, were simply too afraid of the consequences if they tried to get away. Until he knew which scenario Cassie fell into, there wasn't much he could do.

Except observe.

That, he could do.

~*~

Things got busy at the library, and Callie was unable to return to the computers until her lunch hour rolled around. But she was ready. She'd been thinking about it all morning.

Seating herself at the same computer she'd used earlier in the day, Callie brought up the translation program Damian had used. She reminded herself to think of him only as "Mr. Dean." Anything else would admit that she'd seen something in him that definitely interested her, something about which she definitely *shouldn't* have been thinking.

She extracted the sticky note Enid had left in the notebook and typed the two word admonition from it into the translation program. It responded with:

καλή όρεξη! --- good appetite!

Callie stared at the screen for a long moment. "Good *appetite?*"

She recalled a few phrases from her high school French classes, one of which was *bon appétit,* an expression commonly used around the world. Could that really have been what Enid intended?

She took another look at the tiny container with the moon goddess's name on it. The two just didn't make any sense.

Unless... No—surely Enid didn't mean that! The stupid jar contained seasoning?

The little wire harness holding the stopper in place caught her eye. It was long past time for her to find out what was inside. The thought of opening it and tasting the contents crossed her mind, but the prospect of sampling something so old—and so weird—revolted her. Daring had never been a part of Callie's personality. She needed to give it more study.

Turning back to the computer, she looked up the name of the goddess, Achelois.

The machine produced links to a number of articles. Working her way through them, Callie read all she could about the goddess. She soon realized the articles didn't vary a great deal, and the same text often showed up, verbatim, from one website to another.

Short of reading every ancient text that mentioned the lesser moon goddess, Callie settled for what seemed to be a consensus. She learned that Achelois, in addition to being one of the muses who inspired humans to achieve wonders in science and the arts, was also described as "she who washes away pain."

Another source claimed the ancient Greeks made sacrifices to her in hopes of securing her aid in healing the sick and injured. Callie thought that a reasonable assumption since the parents of Achelois were Epione, a goddess who soothed pain, and Asclepius, the god of medicine.

What surprised her as much as what she leaned about Achelois, was her lack of knowledge about the other deities. How had she managed to study "the classics" in college and miss them?

Those thoughts gave way to more practical ones—how to use what she'd just learned. Still not eager to open the Achelois jar and taste the contents, she focused on Enid's comment, "Bon appétit." If intended to be used as a spice, then that's what she needed to do.

"Tonight," she reminded herself, "is spaghetti night. I think I'll just let Theo take the first few bites and see what happens."

Chapter Three

"Computers are like Old Testament gods, lots of rules and no mercy." —Joseph Campbell

Thoughts of revenge provided enough motivation for Theo to make it home. He mentally reviewed one scenario after another in which he triumphed over the three cross-border criminals who had attacked him. And, once he'd dispatched them, he looked forward to doing the same to Wanda.

Being outnumbered three-to-one didn't matter much when it came to daydreams, but the reality of his situation eventually broke through. If he went after them on his own, it would more than likely end up the same way their first encounter did. Once was more than enough.

The bastards didn't fight fair!

He immediately chastised himself for even thinking something so moronic. Nobody fought fair in a bar brawl. What he needed, he decided, was a way to even the sides. Big Lou and Salty would surely want a piece of the guys who beat him up. Maybe what he really needed was a gun. He wondered if either of his friends had one he could use.

Vowing to ask them as soon as he could, Theo limped into the apartment, took a few aspirin and collapsed on the sofa. Callie would take care of him when she got home.

~*~

As Callie prepared to leave for the day, Gail McCrary, the Head Librarian, waved to get her attention. "I'm glad I caught you," she said. "You've got a phone call. It's some attorney's office; they have birthday greetings for you. I had no idea they did that! Why don't you take it in here? I'll be gone for a few minutes. I've got to look for something in the storage room."

Callie thanked her and answered the call. "This is Callie Flynt."

"Please hold for Mr. Parkhurst," said a female voice. She didn't wait for a response.

"Mrs. Flynt? Gordon Parkhurst here. I've got some good news for you."

She recognized his voice but couldn't imagine what he was talking about. "You do?"

"According to our records, you're turning twenty-five tomorrow. Is that right?"

"It is. But how did–"

"Your great aunt left instructions for us to contact you on or shortly before this date."

"Okay, but–"

"I'm pleased to advise that Enid Drummond established a trust fund in your name, and the proceeds can now be made available to you."

Callie assumed the deep breaths she had been taking might have contributed to a bit of lightheadedness. "I had no idea. I– Uh...."

"We'll disperse the proceeds on a monthly basis. The amount may vary from time to time because it's dependent on the revenue the account generates. But I think it's safe to say that for the foreseeable future you may expect to receive about five thousand dollars a month. I'm holding a check in that amount, made out to you, right now."

"Five thousand dollars?"

"Five thousand, two hundred, twelve dollars and sixty-three cents to be exact. Tax-free."

Flabbergasted, Callie stared at the phone as if it were alive. "I don't know what to say."

"You don't need to say anything, Mrs. Flynt. It's obvious your great aunt thinks very highly of you."

"I suppose so."

"Will it be convenient for you to drop by our office? There are some forms I need you to sign. In addition, we have another issue concerning you and Ms. Drummond's estate. She insisted we discuss the matter with you in person. I can come to your home or office if you prefer, or–"

"No. I'll come by your office tomorrow," Callie said. "Have you mentioned this to anyone else?"

"Certainly not," Parkhurst said. "And to be perfectly honest, I wasn't comfortable calling you at your office, but I didn't have a home phone or a cell number on file."

"I'll be getting a cell phone very soon," Callie said, now that she could afford one of her own. Theo claimed he had to keep the one they had in case the union hall needed to reach him for something important. *Like that would ever happen.*

"Since our last meeting, I–" Parkhurst paused and cleared his throat. He sounded uncomfortable. "I'm also… I've been a bit concerned."

"About what?"

"About *who*, actually. I'm referring to Mr. Flynt. I would have brought all this up when you were here earlier, but with him so close… Is there any way you could arrange to visit us by yourself? Until you've had time to fully absorb Ms. Drummond's proposal, you may not want to share the details with anyone else."

"That's fine with me," Callie said, delighted to leave Theo out of her affairs. "I can be there first thing in the morning."

"We open at ten," he said. "We'll have coffee and Danish on hand when you get here."

They ended the call, and Callie sat back in the Head Librarian's chair. Ideas, dreams, and endless possibilities whirled in her brain as she contemplated the freedom she would enjoy with a tax-free income of five thousand dollars a month.

As long as she would be talking to an attorney, she would bring up the matter of a will. And, she decided, she could inquire about a divorce. The trust fund had just given Callie wings. She certainly had no need for an anchor.

~*~

Damian had retraced his steps from the previous day both mentally and physically. If his missing wallet didn't turn up at the library, he could only conclude it had been stolen. He just couldn't figure out how or where it happened.

He hailed the Head Librarian as she passed him on her way to her office.

"How can I help you?" she asked.

"I'm hoping someone turned my wallet in to the Lost and Found."

"You're welcome to check, but I wouldn't hold out much hope. We mostly get things the kids leave behind." She reached under the counter and retrieved an appropriately marked cardboard box. "Have at it."

"Thanks," he said as he combed through what little occupied the container.

"Any luck?"

"Unfortunately, no." He cast a glance at Callie as she exited the Head Librarian's office.

"Happy birthday, Mrs. Flynt!" chirped Ms. McCrary.

"Why, thank you." Callie smiled at her boss then noticed Damian looking at her. "Back so soon?" she asked.

Ah! Her last name's Flint. Gotta remember that. "My wallet's missing. I thought maybe I left it here."

"Oh!" Callie cried. "About that. I found it yesterday, but I forgot to turn it in. I'm so sorry."

"No," he said. "Don't be. It's a relief."

"It's not like you to forget something like that, Callie," Ms. McCrary said. "But, all things considered, it couldn't have been in safer hands." She nodded to them both and continued on her way.

Callie surrendered the billfold with a blush and another apology.

"I'm the one who should apologize," Damian said. "I'm an adult. I ought to be able to keep track of my own stuff." He looked into her eyes, willing himself to avoid even a quick glance at her bruises. "So, it's your birthday?"

"Tomorrow," she said.

"Got any plans?"

She hesitated before responding. "Actually, I do. In the morning. Why?"

In for a penny... He swallowed. "'Cause I'd like to take you to lunch." When she didn't instantly turn him down, he blundered on. "Call it a thank you for saving my wallet."

"I couldn't," she said. "It- It wouldn't be right."

"*Not right?* People go to lunch together all the time." She looked like she might be wavering. He gave her a broad smile. "This is gonna sound really corny, but I know this great little place-"

She chuckled.

"-that has the best sandwiches on Earth. Seriously. Crazy thing is, they only make a few of my favorite: ham and smoked gouda on a pretzel roll." He closed his eyes in a mock swoon. "They're incredible."

"Well, tomorrow is my day off...."

"Excellent! How 'bout I meet you here a little before noon. Okay?"

Uncertainty clouded her sweet face. "Are you sure? I mean-"

"I'm *completely* sure. And I promise you'll love it. But we have to get there before they run out of gouda."

She smiled. "Okay then. Why not?"

∼*∼

On the bus ride home, Callie alternately worried that

Theo would uncover two of her secrets: her lunch date with Damian and her plan to divorce him. On the rare moments when she could contemplate anything else, she dreamed about how she might use some of the money from her trust fund. That, too, had to be kept a secret. With all that spinning through her brain, she gave little thought to the exotic spice she planned to add to the evening meal.

"I'm home," she said as she entered the darkened apartment.

Theo lay sprawled on the couch and groaned in response to her greeting.

"What's the matter?" she asked.

He reached for a table lamp and turned it on, squinting against the suddenly bright light.

Callie gasped when she saw his face. Or what used to be his face. One eye had swollen completely shut, the other resembled horizontal cleavage in a mashed potato. Dried blood crusted his nose, mouth, chin, and one ear.

His blue denim work shirt looked like a Rorschach test rendered in maroon ink.

"What the hell happened?"

"Gang of Mexicans jumped me," he said. "Ambush."

"My God! Where?"

"Toni's place. Bitch set 'em on me."

"Who, Toni?"

"Nah. An old hag she hired as a waitress. I'm gonna sue."

"The waitress?"

"Her, the bar, the Mexicans, all of 'em. I'll own 'em

all—lock, stock, and taco."

Callie shuddered to think what he'd be like as a bar owner. "Did you call the police?"

"No. Not yet. I couldn't. It hurt too much to do anything. Later. I'll call later."

Several empty beer cans littered the floor near the sofa, Theo's version of self-medication. "I see you found the six-pack I bought."

"Yeah. We got any more?"

"I doubt it. Besides, you've had enough. It's time for you to get in the shower."

"Why?"

"Because you're a mess! I won't know if you need to be stitched up until I can see your wounds."

He eased up on one elbow and whimpered. "Gimme a hand?"

She awkwardly supported one side of him while he inched toward their tiny bathroom. Once inside, he sat zombie-like on the toilet while she started the shower and adjusted the temperature. "Do your best to scrub off the dried blood."

"I hurt everywhere," he groaned.

"I imagine so, but you'll just have to tough it out."

"You're a real bitch, ya know that? I– I was hopin' for a little sympathy."

"I *am* sympathetic. I'm also hungry. I'll get dinner ready while you clean up, and I'll bring you something to wear."

"Can ya help me get un–"

"Undressed? No. You're a big boy. Do it yourself." She wondered where and how she'd acquired the ability to show him disrespect, not that she cared. She liked it. He would have cracked her skull open if he hadn't been so badly beaten himself. Boiled down to basics, she liked him better broken and bruised.

"Don't dawdle. I'll have dinner ready soon."

"Whatever," he said, accompanied by a one-finger salute.

"Love you, too." *Maybe he'll slip in the shower and break his neck.* Considering the run of wonderful luck she'd enjoyed that day, it was entirely possible.

When it came time to season the meal, she had no trouble sprinkling his with a goodly dose of the Achelois spice.

With any luck, she thought, it won't kill him.

~*~

Though it took a monumental effort to get in the shower, and the hot water made the cuts sting, the cleansing helped. It even loosened him up a bit. Theo toweled off gently and gazed in the mirror to survey the damage. Having the use of only one eye didn't help.

He leaned closer for a better look at the swelling around his eye. The view reminded him of how some wrestlers looked after a particularly tough match. For some reason, the female fighters never seemed to take such beatings.

Wouldn't want to smear their damn make-up.

If he ever got his hands on Wanda, he'd get to see how bad a broad would look after a beat down. Backing away from the mirror, he raised his hand and tried to make a fist. Something in his arm protested vehemently, and he abandoned the effort.

He reached for the clothes Callie set out for him. "Can ya help me get dressed?"

"I'm fixing dinner."

"It can wait."

"Not if you expect it to be edible. Do the best you can."

He struggled into an Alabama "Crimson Tide" T-shirt and a pair of boxer shorts, groaning with every movement. *Callie prob'ly loves this, loves knowing I'm in pain. Bitch.*

Ignoring the socks and jeans she left on the bed, he made his way into the kitchen and sat in one of two folding chairs at the card table where they usually ate.

A steaming mound of spaghetti waited for him. The aroma drifted up, and even though it came from meatless tomato sauce, he had to admit it smelled pretty good.

She waved a container of parmesan at him. "Cheese?"

"Yeah."

Callie shook a measure of powdered parmesan on his food, and he dug in. After chewing for a while, he commented, "It tastes different."

"New recipe." She watched him eat, her own serving untouched. "What d'ya think?"

"It's okay. Maybe a little better than usual. No meatballs."

"No money."

He glared at her. "What's that s'posed to mean?"

"Just that. I'm outta cash. Can't spend what I don't have. Oh, and by the way, I didn't see the car when I came in. Where did you park? There were a couple open spaces right near the front."

She just never lets up. I'm beat to shit and she's worried about the damned car. "I was too banged up to drive. I'll get it tomorrow."

"If you'll tell me where it is, I'll go get it."

"I *said* I'd get it in the morning! Geez."

"Fine." She stood up, leaving her food to get cold.

"Where you going?"

"To see if we have any bandages for the cuts on your face and arms."

She left the room while he finished eating. He could hear her digging through drawers and cabinets, muttering the whole time. Eventually she returned with an empty box of adhesive strips. "We're out. If you'll give me some money, I'll walk over to the drug store and get some more."

"Never mind," he said, pushing away from the spindly table. "I'll be fine."

"I just don't want you getting blood on the sheets. It's almost impossible to wash out."

He couldn't believe what he'd heard. "You're concerned about the friggin' *sheets?* What about me?"

"Of course I'm concerned about you."

He doubted her sincerity, but there was little he could do about it in his present state. A more pressing issue came to mind. "What's the name of that lawyer we went to?"

"Parkhurst, as I recall."

"You think he'd help me sue the bar and the bitch who hurt me?"

"I thought some Mexicans did this."

"Yeah. I'll sue their asses off, too."

"I don't know if he's that kind of lawyer," Callie said. "I think he mostly handles estates and stuff for rich people."

"Well, he's greedy enough, that's for damn sure." Theo grunted. "I'll bet he'd do it if he thought he'd get enough money out of it."

Callie shrugged. "Maybe. Who knows? You'll have to ask him."

"We'll go see him in the morning. It's your day off, isn't it?"

She hesitated. "We'd probably need an appointment."

Theo laughed and pointed to his swollen eye. "When he gets a load of this, he'll jump at the chance to take the case. I've been thinkin' this through. Toni's smart, and she's been in business for a good while. Knowin' the kind of customers she has, I'll bet she's got a butt load of insurance."

"Hard to say." Callie crossed her arms and looked away. "Insurance isn't cheap. At least, that's what you keep telling me."

"This is different. I could sue for a million bucks. Think of it. One... *million*... bucks. I'll be rich!"

~*~

Though reluctant to leave the comfortable confines of the King George Hotel in Athens, Greece, Enid Drummond knew she had no alternative. She had to move, and keep moving. Doing so while employing multiple identities made it difficult for anyone to find her. Not that she feared just anyone; her concern had a single focus: Aristotle Spanos.

Just thinking of the man gave her a headache. Fortunately, her American attorney, Gordon Parkhurst, had been keeping tabs on the cretin. For reasons she couldn't fathom, he'd somehow managed to worm out of the fifteen year sentence he'd earned in a Federal court after a mere five years. She had hoped he'd serve at least half his sentence. Obviously, a man with his resources could buy his way out of almost anything.

She, however, owned the one thing he would *never* be able to buy, no matter what he offered. Sadly, he knew that, and an offer to purchase what she had would never be forthcoming. Spanos would do anything to get her most prized possession. If he had to kill her in the process, he wouldn't hesitate.

Playing cat and mouse would suffice for a time, but she intended to be ready when a final confrontation took place. Her best option seemed to be finding a way to dictate where and when that might occur.

~*~

Damian awoke in a better mood than he'd enjoyed in ages. The improvement, however, came as no surprise. He'd managed to score a date with Callie and smiled just thinking about it.

Well, he cautioned himself, it's not *exactly* a date in any formal sense, but that hardly mattered. *Just having the chance to get to know her a little better will be enough. For now, anyway.*

He'd spent some time searching the Internet for her street address, and he'd located any number of Flints, but none seemed right. It would have been much easier if he knew her full name. "Callie" sounded like a shortened version of something else. He also found a variation on the spelling of her last name. It could be Flynt. And while he hated to admit it, he might not have heard the librarian correctly. Maybe it was Finch or some other variation.

Except he couldn't find a listing under those names, either. It seemed odd that she could live under the radar. He seriously doubted she'd done it to evade the law. On the other hand, she might be living with someone aiming to do precisely that, someone who wouldn't hesitate to use physical force to keep her in line.

It seemed his only option would be to see where she went at the end of their lunch. He could follow her, discretely, and if she went to a residence, he'd have his answer, assuming she wasn't simply visiting someone.

Why couldn't I have fallen for someone normal, someone who wasn't already married?

He pushed that question out of his mind. Lunch first. Then, he'd focus on finding out who had given her the bruises. After that, who knew?

~*~

Callie hadn't slept well. Her thoughts continually turned to Theo's insistence that they go see Enid's attorney first thing in the morning. She knew Mr. Parkhurst wouldn't say anything in front of him about the trust or whatever else he wanted to discuss. But, damn it, those were exactly the things she *wanted* to discuss. Plus a divorce, and most likely a restraining order, too. Theo would surely go nuts when he learned of her plans.

She got up before he did and made a pot of java. Though not a big coffee drinker herself, she figured a caffeine boost might come in handy. She had just settled into a corner of the sofa when the quiet morning abruptly ended.

"No, no, no!" Theo screamed.

Callie froze. "What's wrong?"

"It's my face. Look at my damn face!"

She hurried to the miniscule bathroom and looked over his shoulder to see his reflection in the mirror. He looked perfectly... normal.

"You look fine," she said. "What's the problem?"

"That *is* the damn problem! Who's gonna believe someone beat the crap outta me if there isn't any swelling. No marks. No cuts. Not even a bruise." Still looking in the mirror, he blinked his eyes. "I can see just fine. Hell, I can see better than I did before."

"That's a good thing, isn't it?"

He turned around to face her. "Whose side are you on?"

"Yours, of course."

He pointed to his face. "Does this mug look like it *got* mugged?"

She shook her head, no.

Tilting his head to one side, he squinted at her, as if trying to read tiny letters on the bridge of her nose. Callie took a step back.

"What'd you do?" He demanded.

"What *could* I have done?"

Once again he waved at his face. "This! Of course. How did you get it to heal so damn fast?"

She hoped she looked as bewildered as she felt. "I swear. I didn't do anything."

"No creams or medicines while I slept?"

"No!"

He continued to point at himself. "How do you explain this, then?"

"Can you hear yourself?" She asked. "You're *blaming* me because you healed faster than you wanted to? That's crazy."

"Oh, now I'm crazy?" He raised his hand to strike her.

"Don't!" she said and backed away as quickly as she could. "I've done nothing wrong. I don't know why you got better so fast. Maybe it's genetic. I've never seen you with a bruise or a cut, so I don't know how long it should take you to heal."

Still angry, he lowered his hand and lumbered into their bedroom.

"I'm sorry things didn't go as you planned," she said, hoping he'd think she was sincere. "Did you still want to go see–"

"Screw you. And your stupid lawyer." He yanked clothing from the closet and quickly dressed.

"Where you going?" She asked.

"None of your damned business," he groused as he walked out the door.

She didn't relax until the door closed behind him, then she smiled. Her prospects for the day had just improved a million percent.

With that thought in mind, she poured herself a bowl of cereal and added a bit of the Achelois powder to the mix.

I'm tired of hiding my bruises. It's time for them to go away. Forever.

Chapter Four

"The poets are the only interpreters of the gods."
—Socrates

Theo had no outlet for his displeasure, and the frustration added fuel to his already smoldering temper. He'd been banged up and bruised in the past, but he'd never healed so fast—ever. The knowledge made him rethink everything he had done the previous day, from the time he'd been attacked until he went to bed that night.

A few things stood out as being unusual, aside from getting his ass kicked by illegals. Having to walk home from Toni's had definitely been a first. There had been numerous occasions when the bartender urged him not to drive, but he'd done it anyway, and nothing had ever come of it.

He'd spent most of the day on the sofa. While that in itself didn't count as odd, the fact that he'd been sleeping most of the time instead of watching TV made it different.

And then there was Callie's reaction to the beating

he'd taken. After her initial surprise, she had seemed pretty callous about it, almost as if she was happy someone had roughed him up. What really stood out as unusual had been her snotty responses to his requests for help. She had never dared to pull that sort of crap before.

Finally, there had been the dinner she fixed. Something about the taste of that spaghetti was definitely different, though he couldn't specifically identify it. He would never be considered some kind of "foodie," but he still had taste buds. For the life of him, however, he couldn't identify the new flavor he noticed in the pasta sauce. He remembered thinking about asking Callie for her opinion, but she didn't even taste the stuff while he had shoveled it in, so he'd abandoned the idea.

The mental review, while not lessening his anger, did give him a target for it: Callie. Nothing else explained his miraculous healing. She did something to his food. She screwed up his plans.

And she would sure as hell pay for her treachery.

~*~

Callie left the apartment building through a service entrance in the back and walked to a bus stop she used only on rare occasions. She had no intention of making it easy for Theo to follow her, as she assumed he would once his outrage cooled enough to let revenge kick in. This time, however, Callie refused to wait around for the inevitable. Thanks to dear old aunt Enid, she had the option to change her life.

She reached the attorney's office where a pleasant, gray-haired woman welcomed her and offered coffee and a sweet roll. Seated in the same conference room as before, Callie dug into the pastry feeling better than she had in months.

Gordon Parkhurst greeted her jovially and handed her a deposit receipt for $5,212.63 along with what looked like a credit card. "I assumed you'd want to open a separate bank account," he said. "So, I took the liberty of setting one up for you." He handed her a pair of documents. "If you'll sign these forms, we can finalize it this morning."

Callie barely heard him. She was busy staring at the receipt in her hand. "If I want to spend some of this money–"

"Use the debit card," said Parkhurst. "Or you can get whatever cash you need from any automatic teller machine in town, or around the world for that matter."

"This is all so amazing," she said. "Theo never let me have money of my own."

Parkhurst frowned. "I suspected something like that, but I didn't want to pry."

"It's time I got a divorce," Callie said. "I'm done with Theo. I want out." In truth, she had been done with him for a long time; she'd just never felt she had a choice in the matter. "Is that something you can help me with?"

"Of course. I'll be happy to handle that."

Force of habit caused her to shield her cheek. "He's going to be furious when he finds out."

The attorney cleared his throat. "I have to ask you this, because I'm concerned about you. Has Theodore ever tried to hurt you?"

Callie responded with a snort of laughter. "I can't tell you how many bottles of makeup I've gone through just to cover the bruises."

"I'm angered but not surprised. Let's also see about getting you a restraining order."

Callie relaxed enough to take another bite of her Danish while Parkhurst continued. "Unfortunately, just having a restraining order in place won't keep you safe. Your best bet is to move somewhere he can't find you. At least for the time being."

"Is there any chance I could move into my aunt's house?" she asked. "I'm sure she wouldn't mind."

A smile lit the attorney's face. "As a matter of fact, Ms. Drummond has been thinking the exact same thing."

"She has? You heard from her?"

"Indeed. I didn't want to mention it until we could speak privately," Parkhurst said. "Not only would she like you to move into her house, she wants you to act as conservator for her collection of religious artifacts. She said you're quite familiar with them."

Stunned by his announcement, Callie looked at the lawyer in silence.

"Ultimately, Ms. Drummond would like to loan her collection to a museum somewhere. She originally thought about opening one of her own, but decided against it."

Callie struggled to take it all in. "What would my job as conservator entail?"

"In a nutshell, you'd take care of her collection until such time as it could be housed somewhere else. She would also like you to head up the search for that place."

"That's it?"

"I believe so. She wants me to handle any legal issues that might arise, but she assured me you would be more than capable of finding a home for her treasures."

"But I don't–"

"There's a generous salary that goes with the job," he added.

Exhaling, Callie sat back in her chair and took a sip of her coffee. It all seemed too perfect, too good to be true. Surely Theo would come crashing into the room at any moment and beat her, and Parkhurst, into the ground.

"Well?" he asked.

She smiled. "Can I start today?"

"I rather thought you'd like the plan." Parkhurst chuckled. "I hope you won't mind, but in addition to everything else, I directed the maintenance company that's been looking after the place to get it ready for an occupant."

"I'll have to go back to the apartment and get a few things," Callie said.

Parkhurst's expression changed dramatically. "If what you've told me about your husband is correct, that might be a bad idea."

"I'm sure I can get in and out when he's not there. He spends a lot of time drinking with his friends. That's when I'll go."

"Please be careful."

"I will," she said. "I will."

~*~

A gentle tone interrupted the late morning breakfast of Aristotle Spanos. A new message had arrived on his cell phone. Updates of this caliber rarely appeared as his subordinates understood the downside of wasting his time. They had also been made keenly aware of the generous rewards given to those who brought him pertinent information. He hoped this would be such.

Temporarily ignoring his lobster frittata and what remained of the caviar piled on top of it, Spanos thumbed the message to life.

Activity at the Buckhead estate. Not just the usual maintenance and ground keepers. Possible new tenant.

Interesting, thought Spanos. Could our dear old Ms. Drummond be planning a return to the deep South? If so, he intended to be ready for her. He set his napkin aside and dictated a response:

Maintain surveillance. Obtain identity of anyone moving in. Advise immediately of any progress.

He made a mental note to have the observer given a bonus, then returned to his meal.

The lobster seemed slightly overdone, so he carefully cut away the exterior to reveal the cream-colored layers inside. A forkful proved succulent and tasty, especially with the caviar garnish. The potato layer which supported the frittata lacked the sort of spices Spanos preferred. But, he reasoned, even the most extraordinary kitchens, manned by chefs of unequaled skill, lacked the spices he desired—the kind he had dedicated his life to finding.

The thought brought him back to the woman who possessed them. He doubted Drummond would be stupid enough to return to her home. She had to know he had someone keeping an eye on it. Even so, whoever did move in might be able to provide a clue to her whereabouts. Whether or not they'd be willing to share such intelligence was another question. He grinned at the idea that unwillingness could make data unavailable.

Such an attitude would only make extracting the information more interesting.

He turned his attention back to his meal which had cooled slightly while he addressed business affairs. After five boring years in custody, he deserved a little something special, so he dialed up the hotel's executive chef, ordered another lobster frittata and told him to exercise more care while preparing it.

Or else.

~*~

His watch showed ten past Noon, and there had been no sign of Callie. Damian sucked on his tenth breath mint, fussed with his collar, patted his hair, checked his nails, his shoelaces, and the zipper in his pants. Nothing could be amiss. Meanwhile, a small herd of fears roamed freely in his head, and the possibility she would intentionally stand him up took precedence. Immediately following came the thought her husband had somehow found out and would try to intervene. That led naturally to the immensely unpleasant prospect of facing the lowlife who had hit her, repeatedly.

Though he hadn't gotten exactly what he'd hoped for from the self-defense book, Damian had come away with an important bit of knowledge. He would rely on it if the need arose, and God willing, it would be enough.

He shook off that thought and let the worry cycle repeat as a thin layer of perspiration formed on the back of his neck. *C'mon, Callie. Hurry up!*

And finally, she appeared.

She waved when she saw him and headed his way. He couldn't help but notice a lightness in her step and the smile on her face. All traces of bruising had disappeared. She looked happy and confident.

What could possibly have caused that? Whatever it was, he agreed with it.

"Hungry?" he asked when she reached him.

"Famished."

"Shall we take my car?"

"It's either that or walk," she said. "My– Uhm. I don't have a car."

He escorted her to his aging but freshly washed Toyota sedan and held the door for her as she slipped inside. They made small talk on the way to the restaurant, and a parking space miraculously appeared close by. Damian wasted no time taking advantage of it. "I've never parked this close before."

"Must be your lucky day," she said.

He couldn't help but smile. *You have no idea.*

Quickly seated inside the neatly appointed café, Damian shared his thoughts on the menu, though they both opted for his favorite.

While chatting over iced tea as they waited for their food to arrive, Callie suddenly frowned. "I thought things had been going too well."

"What is it? What's wrong?"

Clearly agitated, Callie nodded toward a window facing the street. "My husband, Theo, just walked by. I've got to hide. Now!" She stood abruptly and hurried toward the restroom.

Keeping his eye on the entrance, Damian pretended to dine alone. The ruse failed.

"Where is she?" demanded Theo as he slammed the table with his hip.

Though his heart raced, Damian forced himself to ignore the provocation. "Do I know you?"

"You don't *want* to know me, asshole. Now where the hell is she?"

The room went silent as the other diners and the restaurant staff watched the confrontation. No one moved.

"I know she's here, damn it. I saw her get in a car with you at the library."

"You're mistaken. I don't know who you're talking about," Damian said. He took a breath, still feigning calm. "But even if I did, I wouldn't tell you."

Theo leaned in close, his beery breath suffocating. "I'm talking about my wife! Tell me where she is, or I'll beat it out of ya."

Damian eased back and slipped his hand into his pocket to search for his keychain. "That's not a good idea," he said.

"Not for you, anyway."

"I'm warning you," Damian said. "Leave me alone."

"Have it your way, dumb ass!" Theo grabbed Damian's shirt with both hands and yanked him upright.

A strained collar button took flight as Damian pulled a small, keychain-mounted spray bottle from his pocket and brought it close to Theo's face.

"What the–"

Damian leaned away while keeping the dispenser as close to Theo's nose as he could, all the while dosing him with pepper spray.

Theo tried to back away, but Damian grabbed *his* shirt with one hand and kept spraying with the other, bathing his attacker's face, arms, and hands.

"Stop! Enough," Theo blubbered. "I can't see! Oh, sweet Jesus, stop! I can't breathe."

Callie appeared, seemingly out of nowhere. She stood beside Damian and stared down at Theo as he lay on the floor, whimpering and clawing at his eyes. Briefly turning her attention away from Theo, she addressed Damian. "Are you okay?"

He nodded, but whatever nerves he'd kept hidden before suddenly became visible. His hand shook as he lowered the spray bottle to the table. "I didn't have the chance to tell you what I learned from the self-defense book." His voice sounded anything but steady.

She smiled and pointed at the pepper sprayer. "That?"

"Yeah. I'm not much of a street fighter."

Theo continued to groan and grovel, but he managed to open one eye enough to squint up at Callie. "You bitch! When I get–"

Damian kicked him under the jaw. Though swift, the blow wasn't delivered with a great deal of force, merely enough to encourage Theo to choose his words more carefully.

"Somebody call the cops!" Theo gasped between coughs. "He attacked me!"

Damian gestured toward the other diners, all of whom appeared pleased by the outcome of the scuffle. "You're not likely to find much sympathy here. If I give you a wet cloth for your eyes, will you leave quietly? If so, I won't call the police and have you arrested for assault."

"Arrest *me?* I'm the one who just got kicked!"

"I only needed to get your attention, otherwise you'd be out cold. Now, do you want that cloth or not?"

"Yes, damn it. Gimme the cloth. If I go blind, I swear to God I'll sue."

"Just so you know, water won't help much. The effects will wear off in an hour or two, but you need to get that stuff off your hands otherwise you'll just keep rubbing it in your eyes."

Callie emptied her water glass on a cloth napkin, soaked it thoroughly, and dropped it on Theo's hands.

The restaurant manager joined them and assisted Theo who grumbled and cursed all the way to the door.

Callie sat down as activity in the café returned to normal. "Thank you," she said, still on edge as she watched Theo stagger by the restaurant's front window. "Could he come back anytime soon?"

"Not while we're still here." About to rub his face, Damian thought better of it. He needed to wash his hands first. "This isn't what I had in mind when I asked you to lunch."

"I know. I'm sorry. I just–"

He tried to sound reassuring. "Don't worry about it. I'm fine. More importantly, *you're* fine. I hope you weren't planning to go home to that–" he hesitated "–that jerk."

"I'm not."

Damian's heart began to beat nearly as fast as it had when he came under attack. "Listen, if you need a place to stay...."

Callie shook her head. "No, I'm good. All set, in fact. But if you wouldn't mind, I could use a ride to my new place."

"I've got the whole day off," Damian said. "I'll take you anywhere you want to go."

Callie exhaled as if she'd been holding her breath. "You're an angel."

When their meal arrived, she told him about her decision to get a divorce and a restraining order.

"Y'know," he said, "I couldn't have asked for a better dessert."

~*~

Theo made his way carefully down the block until he reached his car. He climbed in, let the seat back, and kept the wet cloth on his face, waiting for the pain and swelling to subside. Much to his surprise, relief came more quickly than he expected.

Chalk it up to whatever that bitch put in my spaghetti. Serves her right. I oughta go back and kick both their asses. Though tempting, he doubted he'd be up to the task before they got away.

He would give her hell when she got home, assuming she ever came back, and that seemed unlikely since she had obviously found herself a lover. With much of his sight restored, Theo started the car and drove the short distance to Salty's place, a basement room he rented from his parents.

Theo pounded on the door until his friend responded. Bleary eyed and sleepy, Salty waved his arm to invite Theo in.

"No time, Salt. I need your help."

"With what?"

"I need to teach my lyin' cheatin' bitch of a wife a lesson."

Salty squinted at him. "You look like shit, man. What happened to you?"

"Long story. I'll tell you later. For now, I need you to get your car. There ain't much time."

"Why my car?"

"'Cause Callie won't recognize it, and we need to follow her."

"*We?*"

"Yeah."

"What's in it for me?"

"C'mon Salty! I need your help. I'll pay ya back. You know I'm good for it. And if she's going where I think she's going, I guarantee there'll be something in it for you, something big. But we gotta hurry."

Salty gave in and the two headed back to the café where Theo last saw Callie. On the way, Theo gave his account of the unprovoked attack by his wife's lover. Salty agreed the bastard needed to be taught a lesson. They continued their righteous journey in silence and double-parked across the street to watch and wait. Minutes later, Callie walked out into the sunshine.

"That's her," Theo growled. "And that guy she's with? He's the chicken shit who hit me with pepper spray."

"We need to squirt it up his ass," opined Salty.

Theo answered with a grim laugh. "We need to give him a bath in it!"

"I feel guilty asking you to drive me around like this," Callie said.

Damian's look discounted the remark. "Why?"

"You only asked me to lunch, and then Theo showed up, and–"

"Forget it," Damian said. "It's not important. I'd rather hear about this place you're moving to. Is it a rental?"

"Hardly," Callie said. "It's my great aunt's house. She lives somewhere in Europe, and she wants me to take care of the place. I'm afraid it's going to be a huge task."

"Big house?"

"You'll see for yourself."

They wove their way through heavy traffic on Peachtree Street to reach Buckhead then headed north, past a number of mansions before taking a side street lined with still more huge homes.

Damian whistled. "You'll be living around here?"

"That's the plan," she said and directed him to a driveway that wound through well-maintained hardwoods and shrubbery. "It's back in here."

Damian pulled to a stop in front of a three-car garage on the side of a building which could have housed multiple families with room to spare. "It's a castle!"

"Can you see me taking care of something this big?"

"It looks like someone's beaten you to it," he said, gazing at the well-tended grounds and freshly planted flower beds.

Callie sat back in surprise. "You're right. The last time

I was here— Well, let's just say I didn't see much of this stuff. But," she added, "it was at night, and I was focused on... other things."

They left the car and approached the front entry, a set of double doors under a wide portico. "This place is amazing," Damian said. "I know you only asked me for a ride here, but...."

"What?"

"Would you mind showing me around a little? I've always wondered how the 'other half' lived. This would give me a little look."

"Of course!" She unlocked the door with a key Parkhurst had given her. "C'mon in. There's no telling what kind of shape the place–" Her comment ended when she flipped on the lights.

Since she ordinarily used a partially hidden side entrance to reduce the chances of being spotted, Callie hadn't been in the formal foyer of the building since her teens.

"Holy cow," Damian said, his voice hushed.

The huge chandelier overhead illuminated a space featuring a massive, curving staircase, marble flooring, and a grand piano.

"Y'know," Damian said, "I wouldn't be surprised to see Fred Astaire and Ginger Rogers dancing down those steps and twirling around in here."

Callie laughed. "I love those old movies, too." She looked at him with renewed appreciation. "Theo would never have watched them."

"Why am I not surprised?"

They continued the tour, though Callie purposely avoided mentioning the secret passageway from the parlor to the special room on the top floor. She focused instead on the opulent rooms downstairs and one or two bedrooms on the middle floor. All were immaculate. None of the sheets which formerly covered the furnishings remained. Floors, walls, windows—everything—sparkled and smelled fresh and clean.

"You did all this?" he asked.

"Me?" She shook her head in wonder. "Not a chance. I spent all my time at the library, remember? Aunt Enid had her attorney take care of it. He must've hired a platoon of worker bees."

She reached for his hand and dragged him toward a rear entrance. "And unless I'm sadly mistaken, they probably did some work out back, too."

Another pair of double doors led to an expansive deck overlooking a swimming pool nestled in a grotto-like setting. Callie grinned as she flipped a switch mounted on the railing. Immediately, water flowed down a small stream through the surrounding boulders and emptied into the pool after pouring over a cliff suspended several feet above the surface.

"I was right. They fixed up the pool, too."

Damian, his hands shoved in his pockets, took it all in. "This is breathtaking. And you grew up here?"

"Unfortunately, no. I didn't even know about this place until I was in high school. My folks didn't talk much about Aunt Enid except to say she married into money, lots and lots of money. I never understood why they wanted nothing to do with her. It didn't make sense. And yet, she always looked out for me. I mean, as much as someone who lived far away could. When my parents died, she paid for me to go to college. That was the last time I saw her."

They sat down in comfortable chairs on the deck and relaxed. Callie felt safe for once and appreciated having someone with whom she could talk without having to mince her words to avoid a beating.

"I was going to tell you how lucky you are," Damian said. "But after our run-in with your husband today–"

"Soon to be *ex*-husband."

"Right. Anyway, it seems to me you've paid your dues."

"We'll see," she said.

Chapter Five

"Ancient societies had anthropomorphic gods: a huge pantheon expanding into centuries of dynastic drama; fathers and sons, martyred heroes, star-crossed lovers, the deaths of kings—stories that taught us of the danger of hubris and the primacy of humility."
—Tom Hiddleston

Theo's anger consumed him. Distracted by it, he and Salty nearly missed the turn Callie and her new boyfriend took. Instead, the two men stopped at the entrance to the property he'd heard about but never visited. Clearly, Callie and her crooked lawyer didn't consider him good enough to enter such a fancy schmancy place. Her lover, on the other hand....

He'd show her!

"Don't go up the drive," Theo said. "I don't want them to know we're here."

"I thought we was gonna mess 'em up?"

"We will, we will. But the time has to be right. For now, I just wanna see what the bitch is tryin' to cheat me out of. We'll find a place to park and sneak back in through the woods."

It required more time than either of them anticipated to find a place to leave the car and even longer to work their way through the forest-like grounds which surrounded the estate, but they eventually reached the back of the building and hid behind a mound of rocks at one end of a swimming pool.

"Damn, man," Salty said, staring up at the imposing structure. "This is like the White House."

"More like the Governor's mansion," Theo said. "Only ritzier." About to say more, he suddenly went silent and hushed Salty with a finger to his lips. "Look," he whispered. "They're comin' out!"

Peering through flowering shrubs which lined a dry streambed leading to the pool, the two listened intently to hear what Callie and her boyfriend discussed. When water mysteriously began to course down the previously empty waterway, it became impossible to make out what they were saying.

"I've gotta get closer," Theo groused. "Stay here. Don't move."

He worked his way toward the patio, using the boulders and thick planting around the pool for cover. Hiding under the patio overhang, he heard Callie correct her lover and refer to Theo as her "soon to be ex-husband."

Theo seethed, his anger triggered even more, and only by sheer strength of will did he manage to stay both quiet and hidden. *Oh, you total bitch! You'll pay for that.*

No longer concerned with the conversation going on above him, Theo turned his thoughts back to the counsel Big

Lou had provided. If Callie inherited all this and died before she could get a divorce, it would all belong to him.

All of it.

He smiled as a new plan began to form. He pulled on Salty's shirt sleeve. "We need to get outta here for now. We'll come back tonight."

"What if they leave?"

"She won't. She has nowhere else to go, and I can take out her boyfriend later."

~*~

The latest text message from the observer Spanos paid to watch Enid Drummond's estate brought much hoped for news. Someone was moving in! The time for action had finally arrived.

While it would have been a great deal less trouble simply to hire someone to extract the information he wanted, it would have deprived Spanos of the opportunity to punish someone himself. He didn't really care who that "someone" might be. After so many years in confinement, he needed the therapeutic lift he'd get from the procedure he had in mind. It had been far too long since he last used it. Fortunately, the corpse he left behind had never been found.

Knowing the coming transformation would require a great deal of energy, Spanos needed to load up on protein and carbohydrates. He also knew he'd be incapacitated until the change was complete. Other issues required planning as well; chief among these were transportation and camouflage. He had to be in place and well-hidden before the change began or the effort would be doomed.

Fortunately, his observer had provided all the necessary information. His driver would take him where he needed to go; the spy gave him an appropriate spot in which to hide, and he'd be able to enjoy himself when night fell. With any luck, he'd obtain the information he'd sought for so long.

He held a small, ceramic jar in the palm of his hand and gazed at the Greek label on it:

Έχιδνα

The ancients, he thought, would be utterly outraged to know how the name of such a delicious monster from their fabled pantheon had been given to a wretched, little mammal from Australia. Of course, the ancients and their gods were gone. At least for the most part.

Spanos checked his watch. He had plenty of time. He just needed to set the process in motion.

~*~

Callie and Damian eventually left the shade of an umbrella on the patio and moved indoors. "I wish I could offer you something to drink," she said, wandering over to a double-door refrigerator. "But as you can imagine, I haven't had time to do any–" She stopped in mid-sentence when she realized every shelf in the appliance bore a load of food.

Damian chuckled. "Mother Hubbard's cupboard it ain't."

Callie's cheeks grew warmer. "This is insane. I promise, I had no idea about any of this. Mr. Parkhurst said he had made arrangements to get the place ready for me, but this… This goes way beyond anything I'd hoped for."

"I don't suppose there's any wine in there," Damian said. "I mean, how would anyone but you know what you like?"

The cool air from the refrigerator felt good. And, she

realized, so did standing so close to Damian who dug further into the chilly depths.

"We're in luck," he said. "There are four different white wines in here. Something for every palate."

"And if you don't like what's in there," said Callie, pointing to a huge wine rack partially hidden by an immense kitchen table, "you can choose from those."

Damian rummaged in the cabinets until he came up with a pair of wine glasses. "What'll ya have?"

"I don't– Uhm, I'm not–"

Damian put the glasses back. "I'm sorry. I didn't mean to rush you into anything."

"No, it's not that," she said. "I can't remember the last time I had a drink of anything that Theo didn't order. That wasn't very often, but on special occasions he might order something for me."

"Surely you experimented a bit in college."

"Not really."

"Well then, it looks like you need to do a bit of sampling." He looked at her and grinned. "Or did you have something else on your agenda for this afternoon?"

He's really got a great smile. She returned it and pulled out the glasses he'd just put away. "Are you any good at opening these things?"

He bumped his chest with a thumb. "You won't find anyone better. At least, not in this house."

Damian proceeded to open three bottles of red wine and three more of white. He brought out additional glasses and poured a taste in each of six of them, one in front of each bottle. "Okay, Madame, let me know if any of these meet with your approval."

Callie lifted a glass and sniffed the contents. "I'm supposed to swirl it around or something before I taste it, right?"

"Why not? Just pretend you know what you're doing. I've operated that way for years."

They whiled away the afternoon tasting not only the original six bottles but several more as well, and Callie found three she liked a great deal.

"Oh, my God," she gasped. "Look at the time!"

Damian turned a wobbly eye toward a wall clock. "Far as I can tell, it's still Wednesday."

She swatted at him with a cloth napkin.

"What?" he asked. "Have you got a hot date or something?"

"It's almost dinner time."

"Unless you were looking forward to dining alone, I could be talked into helping you fix supper for two."

She blinked at him. Who was this guy? *Theo wouldn't have offered to help fix a meal if his life depended on it.* "Seriously?"

"When it comes to food, my dear, I'm *always* serious."

~*~

Finding a store that sold pepper spray didn't present too great an obstacle for Theo, but obtaining a firearm proved much harder. Not only did he lack the funds to buy one, legally or otherwise, he lacked the nerve to try and steal a gun from anyone he knew who did have one. When he asked Big Lou to let him borrow the automatic he kept in his car, the answer evolved rapidly.

"Not just no, but hell no! You ever heard of forensics?" Big Lou asked.

Theo refused to be cowed. "Sure. It's a big thing on TV. You know, like on cop shows."

"Well it's a big thing in real life, too, dumbass. The cops use forensics to identify specific weapons. And when they find out who owns a gun used in a murder, who d'ya think they arrest?"

"I guess that's why so many shooters throw their guns away."

Big Lou's face didn't match the nastiness in his voice. "I wanna get this straight. You're gonna borrow my nine mil so you can shoot your wife and then throw the gun away?"

"Uh–"

"And what's in it for me other than an arrest and jail time?"

"Well...."

"Go pound sand up your ass, Theo. You haven't got the balls to kill anyone, and you wouldn't know how to get away with it if you did."

Salty had been wise enough to remain silent until the two of them left Big Lou's place. "You could just choke her to death," he suggested.

Theo eyed him with disdain. "You ever kill anyone?"

"No."

"Me neither, though I've been tempted."

"So what're ya gonna do?"

Though still foggy on the details, Theo figured he could resolve them as he got to them. "For now we need to make her death look accidental. There's that big pool, and there's sure as hell no lifeguard."

"How do you know she has a swimsuit?"

Theo eyed the man as if he'd just sprouted antlers. "What? Who cares? Can't she just fall in? Geez, Salty. Sometimes I wonder about you."

"So, how we gonna do it?"

"I dunno. Maybe one of us pushes her in, and the other holds her under water."

"So, what's the pepper spray for?" Salty asked after volunteering to do the pushing.

"It'll slow down lover boy if he's still there."

Salty appeared puzzled. "Won't he be able to see what's going on?"

"Not if we spray plenty of that shit in his eyes. I can tell ya that from personal experience."

"But–"

"Chill out, will ya? Let's just see how it goes," Theo said. *Maybe I'll drown you, too.*

~*~

Seated in the back of his limo, Spanos ate on the way to Enid Drummond's Buckhead estate. His focus had to be on quantity rather than quality, and his food selection mirrored his need for protein above all else. Rather than make the food taste even worse, he opted not to add the required spice to it. Instead, he waited until he'd eaten his fill, then mixed a carefully measured portion of the powder in his tea. Once he'd managed to choke all of that down, he ate mint candies to get the taste out of his mouth.

He'd seen photos of Drummond's house and knew exactly what to expect. He did not, however, anticipate how difficult it would be to traverse the surrounding woods to reach the elegant deck overlooking the pool at the rear of the structure.

Cursing his guide all the way, he made sure the fool understood how important it was to conceal their entry and his later exit.

"I don't know precisely when I'll be able to come back out," he told his redheaded companion. "But it will be late, well after dark, and I have no intention of standing around waiting. I'll text you as I'm leaving. Make sure you're back here to pick me up."

"Yes sir," said the lackey.

He eyed the man sternly. "Do *not* be late. I don't handle disappointment well."

The man hurried back the way they'd come and Spanos settled himself under the deck to wait for the change. Once it began he would have a few minutes to disrobe, after that he'd be at the mercy of his surroundings until the transition ended. He had fond memories of the last time he'd done it, shortly before his incarceration. Despite the interim discomfort, he looked forward to what would come. Once complete, his every sense would be heightened, every emotion magnified, every desire within his grasp.

His newly evolved persona would also be hungry. Extraordinarily so.

Spanos crept as far back underneath the expansive deck as he could get. Deep in shadow, he would be impossible to spot by anyone not specifically looking for him. That thought gave him a rare moment of peace and satisfaction as he felt the changes begin.

~*~

They found steaks in the refrigerator and fresh vegetables in the pantry. Working together, they whipped up a meal the likes of which Callie hadn't had in years. Damian, she discovered, had some serious culinary skills.

When they'd eaten as much as they could, and consumed yet another bottle of wine, they left the dishes on the table and returned to the deck. The summer sun had drifted below the tree line, and a few artfully placed lights came on to keep the waterfall and pool visible.

The air felt just cool enough to be comfortable, and Callie had no illusions about her sobriety. She'd never had quite so much to drink. Yet, she felt in control as well as being relaxed and happy, more so than at any time during her marriage. She liked being with Damian, and any feelings of guilt she might have had disappeared with the knowledge that her divorce would soon be a reality.

"More wine?" Damian asked.

"My dear sir, are you trying to get me drunk so you can take advantage of me?"

He drummed his fingers on the armrest of his deeply padded deck chair. "You want the truth?"

"Of course."

"Then... yes!" He smiled.

"So, so subtle," she said, trying hard not to slur her words.

"That's me."

Callie felt a tickle of inspiration. "I've got an idea. Let's go for a little swim."

"Here? *Now?* We don't have any suits. At least, I certainly don't."

She shrugged. "Who needs 'em?"

"Please tell me you're not kidding," Damian said, his expression puppy-like.

"Considering everything we've found in this house that I never imagined would be available, there just might be some swimsuits tucked away somewhere. What d'ya say we go look for 'em?"

"And if we *can't* find any?"

She giggled, more than a little captivated by the idea of skinny dipping with a man she'd been around for less than a day. "Maybe we'll just have to do without."

~*~

Theo and Salty once again trekked through the woods aiming toward their hiding place behind the pool's water feature. Though harder to see in the gathering darkness, the trail seemed clearer for some reason, as if someone else had recently used it. Salty commented on that, but it didn't make any sense to Theo who told him to shut up.

"Such a grouch," Salty snapped back.

"Gimme a break, will ya? I need to concentrate. Let's just go and get this done."

They continued to make their way through the heavily shadowed trees and the accompanying undergrowth which, after a while, seemed much thicker than before.

"It wasn't this hard when we came through here last time," Salty said.

"I think we got off the damned path," groaned Theo.

Salty tapped him on the shoulder. "Doesn't matter. We're okay. I can see some lights." He pointed them out, and they blundered on, mindful of the thorny plants blocking their way.

~*~

Santos awoke, feeling the power in his new body. His hair had grown dark and long. His arms had become smooth, his skin silky. His stomach, once overlarge and ugly, now had the firm, flat lines of an athlete. He put his hands on his chest and marveled at perfectly formed breasts and taut nipples.

Arching his back, he drew himself upright, nearly bumping his head on the underside of the deck. Rather than remain hidden and with limited sight lines, he slithered out and into the pool. The water allowed for much greater freedom. In addition, he could float his lower body along the sides of the pool. In the limited light, he would appear to be a mortal and undeniably desirable woman.

As long as he remained in the pool, no one would be able to see the long serpent tale into which his legs had grown and which gave him vast strength and great speed.

Nor could anyone see his sharp, pointed teeth until they were revealed in a smile.

Or a bite.

He reveled in his new appearance, temporary though it would be. And despite all the eating he'd done while traveling to Enid's house, one additional issue loomed large.

His buxom new persona craved a live meal.

~*~

Theo and Salty slowed as they approached the pool and quietly reassumed the spots they had occupied previously. The view, however, had changed dramatically. A stunning, nude woman stood in the pool.

"Oh. My. Gawd," Salty breathed, his eyes riveted on the statuesque brunette. "Is– Is that your *wife?*"

"Hell no," Theo said, his mind whirling. *Who was this? Where had she come from? What did she....*

Shifting her body to face them directly, the woman extended her arm and gestured for them to join her with a curled finger.

"Holy shit," gasped Salty, emphasizing each syllable. He immediately pulled his T-shirt over his head.

Theo halted him. "What the hell are you doing?"

Salty stared at him, astonished. "What the hell do you *think* I'm doing? I'm gettin' in the pool with her. She's beggin' me for it!" He stuck his chin toward the woman as he unbuckled his belt.

She continued to look at them, a curious expression on her face. She then lifted one breast in each hand as if inviting a closer inspection.

Salty's jeans hit the dirt, but his feet became tangled as he tried to step out of them. Dropping to the ground, he untied his shoes and freed himself while Theo watched, his mind still racing.

Where was Callie? And who–

He looked up in time to see Salty's pale, naked body sail through the air into the water. The splash muffled his laughter.

What could this gorgeous babe possibly see in his stupid, skinny friend? It made no sense. Stunned, Theo watched as the two embraced.

Salty's arms went around the woman briefly while she held him close. But instead of a long sensuous hug, Salty began to squirm and push against her shoulders to get away. The woman didn't let go, and while Salty writhed and grunted, she looked past him, her eyes locked on Theo.

Confused and frightened, Theo started forward to help his friend when Salty appeared to break free. He managed to put a few feet between his body and the woman's when a massive tail, like that of giant boa constrictor coiled around him.

Salty managed a thin cry for help, his face contorted by fear and pain as the coils encircling him contracted.

Theo froze.

The woman continued to stare at him for a moment then turned her attention to Salty. "Where is Enid Drummond?" she asked, her voice mellow and dusky.

Salty struggled to respond. "Can't– Can't breathe."

The coils surrounding him appeared to relax, and the woman repeated the question.

"Enid *who?* I don't know any–" The coils tightened again, choking off Salty's reply.

Theo looked around for a weapon of some kind but came up empty. Then, remembering the pepper spray in his pocket, he extracted it and hurried toward his friend in the pool, struggling in the grasp of a monster.

The woman brightened when she saw Theo approach and smiled, her teeth pearly white, glistening, and filed into sharp points. Theo halted at the edge of the pool, not sure how to spray her without also spraying his friend.

Salty's eyes rolled in his head, his face had turned tomato red. "Now," he mouthed. "Do it!"

Theo pressed the spray button as the woman drifted closer, her jaws wide. Theo aimed for her mouth remembering all too well how he'd not only been blinded, but choked. Precious air had been denied him. Now it was her turn. He kept spraying.

The bitch in the water, however, enjoyed the spray. She curled her long tongue over shark-like teeth to lick it from her lips. Her eyes never even watered.

"Where is Enid Drummond?" she asked him. "Tell me, or this one dies."

"*Aunt* Enid?"

"Tell me!"

"But– I don't know!"

"So be it."

Salty made a small gurgling sound as the woman pushed his head to one side and took an enormous bite out of his throat and chewed on it.

Theo's stomach convulsed as he backpedaled from the bloody nightmare in front of him. "Salty!"

"Not very," said the woman, taking another bite. A stream of gore cascaded down her neck and trickled between her breasts.

Theo struggled to move feet and legs suddenly grown heavy. Though his mouth had gone dry, his pants felt warm and wet. His fists ached from being so tightly clenched.

"Talk to me," she said, her mouth still full. She let Salty sink to the bottom of the pool. "Now!"

Enthralled by the serpent woman, Theo remained motionless as she moved closer to him, her tail undulating hypnotically in the water.

Forcing himself to break free of her spell, Theo turned and sprinted away. He tripped on Salty's discarded clothing but righted himself with an almost inhuman effort. He could hear the vile thing coming after him, still chewing and likely gaining speed.

He knew what his chances were if she caught him. The knowledge gave him speed he never knew he had.

~*~

As Callie and Damian searched through one bedroom after another, her conscience battled with her desire. What on Earth was she doing? Could she blame it all on a little wine? *Okay, maybe more than a little wine.* But still, was she seriously prepared to strip naked and jump into a swimming pool with a man she hardly knew?

"Yes!" She told herself. *Yes in-damn-deed!*

When they had checked every possible spot where someone might have stored a swimsuit, they gave up and returned to the kitchen.

"Listen," Damian said, "if you aren't comfortable with this–"

Callie gave him a nervous laugh. "I just don't want you to think I'm some terrible kind of person. I've never done anything like this before. Ever!"

"Neither have I. Does that make *me* a terrible person?"

"Of course not."

"Then why would it be any different for you?"

His logic seemed reasonable, but she knew the wine had to be influencing her. How modest could she appear standing bare naked in front of him? "How 'bout we turn out the lights first, before we get undressed?"

"To be completely honest," he said, "I'd prefer it that way myself."

Callie approached the row of light switches beside the double doors leading to the huge redwood deck. With a minimum of experimentation she located the ones needed. "I'll leave a couple on around the pool, just enough to navigate. She returned to his side, took a deep breath, and reached for his hand.

"You ready?"

He gave her the kind of smile Theo once beamed at her long ago. She missed that smile more than she could say. *Theo, not so much; not at all, in fact.* She couldn't even guess how long it had been since she'd gotten over the infatuation which led to their marriage.

Damian swallowed and squeezed her hand. "I'm as ready as I'll ever be."

He walked beside her but stopped when they reached the kitchen table still laden with dinner dishes. "Hang on a sec." He released her hand and grabbed two wine glasses and the last bottle they'd opened, a rich, red port.

"Liquid courage?" she asked.

"Yes, ma'am."

Together they walked out into the calm, cool night, nervous, but unafraid.

Chapter Six

"Now, as of old, the gods give men all good things, excepting only those that are baneful and injurious and useless. These, now as of old, are not gifts of the gods: men stumble into them themselves because of their own blindness and folly."—Democritus

Spanos cleared the edge of the pool, but lost sight of his target as the man sprinted behind the faux waterfall. The rocks behind and at the base of the water feature bit into his skin as he slithered after his prey.

He worked his way to the grass where he could move faster and continued the pursuit. With his enhanced senses, there would be no mistaking his target's whereabouts. In his present form, Spanos could see in the dark nearly as well as he could in daylight. That would definitely work to his advantage when chasing the idiot into the woods.

Except the idiot *didn't* enter the woods as anticipated. Instead, he raced around the backyard toward the side of the house, vaulting over a fence in the process.

Spanos had the option of knocking the fence down or crawling over it, but the obstacle would slow him down no matter which option he chose.

Knowing he'd have to return and retrieve his things without alerting anyone else to his presence, he left the barrier intact and crawled over it. The man he pursued rounded the far corner of the house as Spanos dragged the last length of his tail into the side yard beyond.

Back on grass, Spanos pushed himself to greater speed and gained on the man ahead of him. The sheer act of moving with such a graceful and coordinated body invigorated him; the prospect of extracting the information he wanted justified it. But most of all, he hungered for the taste of more human flesh, and his desire for it propelled him to even greater speed.

As he left the side yard, dodging trees and shrubbery, he caught sight of the man once again. He had altered course once more, this time running down the curving driveway.

Spanos followed him but quickly discovered the surface of the drive slowed him down. The blacktop retained the summer heat, and particles of asphalt stuck to his belly as he crawled. The constant contractions of tail muscles which thrust him forward and the weight of his human form pressing down, caused a multitude of painful cuts and breaks in his skin.

Swearing, Spanos moved back to the grass which quickly disappeared when the drive entered the woods surrounding the estate. The man was getting away!

That knowledge, linked with the tingling sensation which heralded the inevitable return to his normal human form, caused him to abandon the chase.

A new thought occurred to him as he cursed himself

for not obtaining his quarry's identity. The first victim's clothing remained by the pool. Surely that would reveal a wallet and ID or some other clues. He could use whatever he found to look for known associates. Surely he'd find some, and he'd have fun *encouraging* them to share his target's whereabouts.

Spanos slithered back around the house and returned to the rear of the waterfall. There he poked through the dead man's clothing and secured his wallet.

As he examined the paltry contents, most of the outdoor lights clicked off. He looked around for some sort of explanation, then heard the doors to the wooden deck open. Perhaps he'd get the answers he sought sooner than he thought.

Pleased with this new possibility, Spanos continued on to the underside of the expansive deck and curled up in the dark to wait.

~*~

Theo's lungs hurt; his throat was raw; pain laced his feet, knees, and hips, but he kept running. There would be no slowing to catch his breath, no time for recovery of anything. If the monster caught him, he'd be dead. Just like Salty—crushed, and eaten.

Dead, and forgotten.

Once clear of the mansion's grounds, he turned his steps uphill toward the spot where they'd hidden Salty's car. If he could just reach it and crawl inside, the hideous thing chasing him could be locked out, assuming it didn't crush the car with him inside.

With the car nearly in sight, he reached into his pocket for the keys. Salty's keys. Which, he finally realized, were in Salty's pants, not his own.

His hopes dashed, Theo cast a hurried look behind to see how much ground the creature had gained on him.

Only, the street looked clear. No creature at all.

Theo slowed, fearing trickery of some kind. Had the monster circled around and gotten ahead of him somehow? That didn't seem likely, unless it knew where they had left Salty's car.

He shook that thought off. It seemed preposterous, as preposterous as being locked out of the only vehicle that might have carried him away to safety.

As his breathing slowly returned to normal and his heart no longer threatened to burst from his chest, Theo examined his options, limited though they were.

He couldn't simply walk home; the drive over had taken most of an hour.

Go back to the mansion? He wouldn't do that if Cassie had access to a dozen cars.

Call someone else?

Big Lou's name came instantly to mind. He needed to talk with someone who could help him sort out all the bizarre shit he'd just gone through. Lou would know what to do, he had to. He could also advise if calling the cops made sense. Would anyone believe him?

But then, he had to do something about Salty. The poor schmuck didn't deserve to die, and he sure as hell didn't deserve to be eaten by something out of a horror movie.

Theo pulled out his flip phone and dialed his friend who answered on the seventh or eighth ring. "No, damn it. I'm not going to let you borrow my gun. And it ain't for sale, either."

"Well it sure would've come in handy," Theo said. "If I'd had a gun, Salty might still be alive."

"What? Salty's dead? How?"

"That is a long, long story."

"I've got time."

"Thing is, Lou. I don't have much time. There's something after me, or at least there was. I'm not sure where it is now. But what I am sure of is that I can't stay here."

Lou exhaled in exasperation. "Where are you?"

"Buckhead."

"If you want me to drive all the way over there, asshole, you'll need to be a little more specific."

Theo gave him the name of the street, but he had no idea what the house number might be. "Just drive down the road. You'll see me, unless–"

"Unless, what?"

"Unless the thing gets me."

"Geezus, Flynt! What the hell are you talking about?"

"You're not gonna believe me," he said. "I'll tell you about it when you get here. On the way back. When I'm… When we're *both* safe."

"Have you completely lost your mind?"

"Maybe," Theo said. "Hell, I don't know. I'm scared is all, scared worse than I've ever been. That thing, whatever it is, killed Salty and it came after me, too. I'm tellin' ya, Lou, I've gotta get outta here now. Right now!"

"Okay, okay," Lou said, his voice signaling resignation. "I'll be there as soon as I can."

"Thanks, man."

"You'll owe me for the gas."

"Just hurry. Okay?"

~*~

With the deck lights out and very little illumination from the kitchen windows, Damian could just make out Callie's slender shape as she set their folded towels aside.

As if by some hidden signal, they both removed their clothing. His thoughts had already completed a cross-country marathon of conflict and wonder, beginning with his mental turmoil over asking Callie to join him for lunch.

Had that just been today?

And now this?

He thanked heaven repeatedly for whatever karma allowed him to not only spend time with a wonderful and attractive young woman, but do so in such a sensually charged manner. In a very few moments he would escort her to the pool, naked. They would get in the water, naked. They would face each other, naked. That alone was enough to arouse him. He hoped the darkness would camouflage his uncontrolled reaction.

Maybe if I think of something stupid....

It didn't work.

From a few feet away Callie giggled. God, how he loved that sound.

"I'm ready," she said.

"Me, too." He glanced in her direction, barely able to see her attempting to cover flesh he guessed was rarely, if ever, exposed.

He poured them each a glass of wine and received a nervous kiss on the cheek as his reward.

"I can't believe I'm doing this," she whispered. "It feels so... so...."

"Sexy?"

She giggled again. "Well, yeah. That."

"C'mon." He took her hand, and they walked down the broad, cedar stairway to the pool deck. "Want me to go in first?"

"Yes," she said. "No! Wait. Let's do it together. We can go in slowly, side by side."

The pool had no deep end and appeared to have been formed by shoving together two kidney-shaped pools of different sizes. The couple set their glasses down and descended the first of two central steps into the water.

"Holy moly!" Callie exclaimed. "It's way colder than I thought it would be. My goose bumps have goose bumps."

Damian tried not to look too long or hard at his companion knowing full well it would add to his condition. To his great relief, the cold water accomplished what his efforts to think of something stupid had failed to do. "Let's keep going. We'll get used to it pretty quick."

"I hope so!"

One more step brought them to the shallow bottom; the water barely covered their knees. "The way I see it, we've got two options," he said. "We can either tough it out and fall in right here–"

"Or?" Despite the dim light, he could see she eagerly wanted to hear another option.

"Or we walk slowly into the deeper water."

Callie looked down. "It's so dark! I can barely see my feet."

"You're not scared, are you?"

She squeezed his hand. "No. At least, not very."

"Look up," he said. "The stars are amazing."

She followed his suggestion. "It helps that there's no moon out tonight."

He gently shifted her chin toward his own. "The stars aren't the only amazing thing I see this evening."

They came together in a gentle embrace, and with Callie's warm body pressed close, they kissed. Damian uttered another silent prayer of thanks. He could never have imagined his luncheon date culminating in anything remotely close to this.

Callie pulled slightly away but kept a tight grip on Damian's forearm. "Let's keep moving."

The depth slowly increased until it barely covered Callie's breasts. "Enough," she said. "I can't stand doing this piecemeal."

With that she dropped completely under water where she remained only for a moment, then burst up laughing and shivering. "Do it!" she said, breathlessly. "Go on!"

Damian followed suit, the water somehow colder than he expected. Like Callie, he stayed under for a second or two then stood bolt upright. "Geez, that's cold!"

"Didn't you tell me we'd get used to it?"

"I said that?" He laughed. "Can't imagine where I got that idea."

"Let's keep moving," she said. "Maybe that'll help."

They continued to plod along in the dark until Callie took a sharp breath and came to a sudden stop.

"What's wrong? Did you forget something?"

"No," she said, a tremble in her voice. "I stepped on something."

"Like a rock or a–"

"Something soft, like… like an arm."

"*An arm?*"

"Yes!" she yelled. "I'm getting out!"

She turned and splashed back toward the steps they'd traversed earlier. Damian barely kept up with her. They left the water, raced around the pool and up the stairs to the redwood deck.

Callie grabbed the towels and threw one to him. "We've got to call the police."

"Are you sure you stepped on… an arm?"

"Or a leg. Hell, I don't know." She wrapped herself in a beach towel and hurried toward an electrical box mounted on the wall. "We can't see anything." She opened the box and flipped all the switches inside, flooding the pool and the surrounding area with bright light.

A man lay face down and motionless at the bottom of the pool. Pink swirls of thinning blood drifted from away from his neck, dispersed by the water.

"Who is it?" asked Damian.

"I have no idea. A worker, maybe?"

"Wouldn't we have seen him earlier, when we sat out here on the deck?"

"You're right. We would have. I'm sure I would have,"

Callie said.

Her voice held steady in contrast to her earlier trepidation. Damian found that both impressive and reassuring. There was a great deal more to her than he might have thought had he not tried to befriend her.

"I'll call 911," he said. "They'll know what to do."

~*~

Theo fidgeted and cursed the delay while waiting for Big Lou to arrive. Try though he might, he couldn't get the grisly scene he'd witnessed out of his head. It kept replaying, over and over, like a short piece of horror film. He paced uphill and down in the middle of the road, unwilling to go near the woods on either side for fear of finding the snake woman lying in wait for him.

He saw few cars, and the darkness magnified every sound. When his friend finally stopped and picked him up, Theo got in quickly and locked his door. They hadn't driven ten feet when he broke down and wept.

"Geez," Lou said. "What's going on? I've never seen you like this."

Theo sniffed and wiped his tears on the sleeve of his T-shirt. "Salty's dead, man."

"So you said on the phone. What the hell happened?"

"You aren't gonna believe this, but I swear it's the truth. There was this woman in the swimming pool–"

"Back up," Lou said. "Start from the beginning."

Theo did his best to recount everything he and Salty had done since his earlier phone call when he tried to borrow Lou's handgun. When he got to the part about the woman in the water, Lou had him slow down. "So, this chick in the pool, what'd she look like?"

"She had dark hair and big boobs, but she wasn't fat. She looked like one of the women wrestlers."

"So, good lookin'?"

"Yeah, real good looking. Until she showed her teeth. They looked... awful. Like the mouth on one of those nasty eels with the sharp teeth we saw on TV."

"A moray eel?"

"Yeah. That kind. She took a bite outta Salty's neck. I swear to God. She just ripped out a huge chunk of meat and chewed it up. I thought I was gonna puke."

Lou shook his head in astonishment. "Then what happened?"

"When I couldn't answer her stupid question, she came after me!"

"What was the question?"

"She wanted to know where Callie's aunt was. How the hell am I supposed to know that? Like I told you, I think the old bag's dead. We haven't heard from her in years."

"So, this crazy cannibal babe climbed outta the pool and–"

"She didn't climb, she crawled."

"Crawled?"

"Well, more like slithered."

Lou cleared his throat. "That's the part I don't get. She was half woman and half boa constrictor?"

"I swear it, Lou. On my mother's grave. You gotta believe me."

Lou sniffed, then sniffed again. "Did you pee your pants?"

"Huh? Yeah, I guess I kinda did." *As if I didn't feel miserable enough already.* "But you would have, too."

They drove in silence for a long while before Theo asked the question that had been bothering him since he got away from the she-monster. "Do you think I should call the cops?"

Lou appeared to mull the question over before responding. "Yeah, I guess you should. I mean, how else will anyone find out who killed Salty? I'd like to think he'd do the same for us if we got murdered."

"Sure," said Theo. "I can call 'em as soon as I get home, but they're not gonna believe me. It's just too fucking strange."

"I'm sure they've heard strange stories before."

"Not like this they haven't." Theo tried to focus on the traffic, the people walking along the streets, business signs, sounds, anything to get his mind off the scene in his head of Salty and the monster who killed him.

"It doesn't matter if they don't believe you," Lou said.

~*~

Spanos opened his eyes and looked out from beneath the deck. He observed a great deal of light and activity, the opposite of what had been going on when he crawled into his hiding place. He regretted not having the opportunity to interrogate the couple he'd seen earlier, but obviously, he fell asleep when the transformation to his own body began.

The air seemed much chillier than it had when he wore the persona of Echidna, and he dressed himself as rapidly as his tight quarters allowed. It wouldn't do to be found naked and in hiding by police who had to be investigating the dead man in the pool. Spanos resisted the urge to laugh; the fools would never figure it out.

They have no chance against me! I'm unstoppable, superhuman. I'm a god. Better yet, I'm any god I wish to be!

He recognized the lie, and he desperately missed feeling the power of Echidna, power he had only been able to borrow for a short time. Though it left him weak and disgusted by his own pitiful abilities, he knew he could perform the transformation a few more times before the supply of spice ran out. Forever.

That thought saddened him, but it also renewed his determination to obtain the rest of the collection. Only one other person knew about and understood the fabulous spices and the powers they bestowed on those who used them. He had to find her soon; they were both growing older.

Someone swept the beam of a flashlight through the darkness under the deck.

Spanos called out in his best imitation of a prison guard, "Knock it off, will ya? I don't need anyone shining a light in my face while I'm working. I'll finish inspecting the area as fast as I can. Now gimme some space!"

He waited for the inevitable grumbling that followed, but he'd played the game enough to know there was little chance anyone would discover his ruse and call him out.

Working his way toward the edge of the deck, he waited until the bulk of the investigatory efforts took place near the waterfall and the body, now being photographed in great detail.

At the appropriate moment, he slipped out from under the deck and walked around the side of the house and out of view. He used speed dial to reach his accomplice and told him to drive up to the mansion, or as close as he could get.

Spanos would be waiting for him.

The police didn't leave until well after 3AM, and Damian remained at Callie's side the whole time. When the last of the police cars, the ambulance, and other assorted vehicles finally departed, Callie collapsed in a living room chair. Though exhausted and feeling the after-effects of too much wine, Callie couldn't relax.

She looked at an equally exhausted Damian sitting in a nearby armchair. He managed a weak smile. "This has been the weirdest damned lunch date in the whole history of lunch dates."

Marveling at how he could always find words to lighten her spirits, Callie blew him a kiss. "I have no idea how any of this happened. It just– I'm...."

"Worn out?"

"Dead."

"No, actually, that was the guy in the pool."

His rejoinder generated only sadness this time. "That poor man." Callie rubbed her eyes. "I just don't understand. Who was he, and how did he end up in the pool?"

"Let's think about it," Damian said. "What's changed in your life? What big thing?"

Callie wondered if she could count them all. "Where do I start? Filing for divorce? Hearing from someone who's been out of touch for years? Moving into a mansion?" A wall clock behind her struck the half hour. "Oh, Lord. Look how late it is. I have to work tomorrow."

"You mean today. I do, too."

"I don't even know what you do," Callie said, embarrassed by the gap in her knowledge.

"I'm an illustrator."

"Like, for textbooks?"

Smiling, he shook his head. "I mostly do children's books or marketing material for them. Sketches and cartoon stuff. It's not great art, and my folks keep telling me I'm wasting my talent. But, to be honest, you can't waste what you don't have."

"Don't be so hard on yourself. Do you enjoy it? I think it'd be fun, but then I can't draw a straight line." She stretched and yawned. "At the library, I loved watching kids getting excited about the books they found in the children's section."

"That's one of the reasons I go to the library so often. I like to see which books get the most attention."

"You could've asked me!"

"I thought about it, and a hundred other ways to strike up a conversation. I didn't want you to think I was stalking you or something."

"I would love to help. It sounds so much more interesting than my job."

Damian rubbed his eyes. "It's pretty boring at times. But it pays the bills, and I can work from home. Not having to commute in Atlanta traffic is a godsend."

"Well it sure beats what I do. Did I mention I'm going to quit the library? My great aunt is paying me to live here and look after her stuff."

"I'm happy for you, but who's going to help me find what I need in the library?"

"Call me," said Callie. "I owe ya."

Damian yawned. "I'm sorry. It's a struggle to keep my eyes open."

"Then stretch out here and go to sleep." She patted the sofa. "Or better yet, use one of the eight million bedrooms upstairs."

"Seriously?"

"Yes. You shouldn't drive, *anywhere*. You're just as tired as I am. And besides–"

"What?"

"I'm frightened. With everything that's happened here tonight... I– I don't want to be alone." She hugged herself as if a cold breeze had blown through the room. "Is that stupid?"

"No. Of course not."

She raised her hands, palms out. "I just want to sleep, that's all. But, if you wanted to stay in the room with me...."

"I could be talked into that. Think of me as your watchdog." He chuckled. "A very tired and sleepy one."

As Callie mounted the stairs she realized she had yet to pick out a bedroom to call her own. Fortunately, she remembered which one had the largest bed when they went looking for swimsuits earlier.

Taking Damian's hand, she confidently led him in that direction.

Chapter Seven

"In ancient times cats were worshipped as gods; they have not forgotten this." —Terry Pratchett

Detective Alice Campbell of the Atlanta Police Department needed a vacation. Her head hurt; her feet hurt, and more than anything else, her back hurt from sitting hunched over in front of a stupid computer screen all day. Every day. For the past 29 years.

When her phone rang, she eyed it with disdain. No one called her this early in the day with good news. But then, as far as she could recall, no one *ever* called her with good news.

She answered the phone with a less than enthusiastic, "Campbell."

"Yo, Campy! I got a live one for ya."

She recognized the crusty voice of fellow detective, Syd Abramowitz, a man she considered a part time moron and full time practical joker, just not a very good one. "I'm not in the mood for any of your shit right now, Syd."

"Lighten up, Campy. I think you'll get a kick outta

this one."

"I can only imagine. What've you got?"

"You heard about the body we pulled outta that swimming pool in Buckhead last night, right? Well, there's a guy in Interview Three who says he witnessed the murder."

Campbell sat up straighter, though she remained suspicious. "And you want *me* to talk to him?"

"Well, yeah. After all, you're the resident shrink. Everyone knows you're the best when it comes to chatting up crazies."

She drummed her fingers on the desk, once again regretting she'd ever mentioned taking abnormal psych classes in college. "Go on."

"Cap'n wants you to talk to him. See if you can figure out if he knows anything we can actually use. You know, real stuff."

"Why d'ya think he's crazy?"

"You'll see," Abramowitz said. "Then you can tell me."

Alice hung up on Abramowitz and grabbed her notepad. She proceeded down the short hallway to the interview room and walked straight in. The man waiting for her looked a bit disheveled and needed a shave but bore none of the traits typically described as wild or crazy. Casually dressed in jeans and a University of Alabama T-shirt, he appeared to be in his late twenties.

"I'm detective Campbell," she said. "I understand you have some information about a murder in Buckhead last night."

"That's right."

She turned on the desktop computer and logged in.

"I'll need a little information before we get into your statement, starting with your name and contact information." She hurried through the preliminaries, typing notes and filling out an on-screen form as she went. "Spell your last name for me, please."

"F-L-Y-N-T. With a 'Y' not an 'I'. Flynt, Theo Flynt."

"Okay, got it," she said, "Thanks. Now, Mr. Flynt, tell me what you saw. Don't leave anything out."

She let him ramble and tried not to interrupt too often, but when he claimed the killer was half woman and half snake, she hit the brakes. "I hate to do this to you," she said, "but I've got a minor emergency I need to handle. If you'll just sit here for a minute, I'll be right back."

When he agreed, she left the room and closed the door behind her. After taking a few deep breaths, she arched her back then bent forward and touched the floor. Her spine made a slight cracking sound, but it heralded a modest amount of relief. She'd been to the doctor about it, and he'd prescribed various things, but she hated the idea of relying on drugs. She'd worked with too many addicts. Like, quite possibly, the guy in the interview room. After another deep breath she went back to work.

"Okay," she said, restarting the conversation as she resumed her seat by the computer, "what did this woman look like?"

Alice remained alert for clue words, facial expressions, or gestures—any hint that the man was doped up or drunk. He didn't seem to be either, and his pupils did not appear dilated, always a good sign.

"How tall was she?"

"I dunno," came the reply. "She was in the pool, and I don't know how deep it is."

"Right. And she had the tail of a snake. What kind of snake?"

"How the hell would I know? I'm no snake expert. I see one; I kill it. But not that one, with or without a broad attached. All I do know is this: a big ass snake wrapped itself around my friend and choked the shit out of him."

"And killed him?"

"No! The *bitch part* killed him when she bit a chunk outta his neck. You're the third cop I've talked to. How many times do I have to say it?"

"I'm sorry, Mr. Flynt. I know it's aggravating to have to repeat yourself, but I need to be absolutely sure I completely understand the information you're sharing. So, please bear with me."

He crossed his arms. "Yeah, okay. Whatever."

"Thanks. Now, you said she bit his neck and drew blood, is that right?"

He exhaled wearily. "No. I said she bit a *chunk* out of his neck. A big damn chunk. Like a bite out of a burger. She came away chewing a big piece of his throat. She did it twice, but I'm pretty sure the first one killed him."

"That must have been a terrible thing to see," she said.

"It was a helluva lot worse for Salty."

"Salty?" She took a moment to look at the computer screen. "According to the DMV, the deceased's name is Abner Bowden."

"We called him Salty." He gave a snort of laughter and shook his head. "Abner, huh? No wonder he liked the nickname we gave him."

Alice made a note of it. "I'm curious. How did you and

Mr. Bowden happen to be in the Drummond's backyard last night?"

"Drummond? Oh, yeah. The old lady who owns the place. She's my wife's aunt."

"Go on."

"I was there to... uh, visit."

Alice hurriedly scanned the case notes on her computer. "That's really odd. For some reason, your wife didn't say anything to the on-site investigator about having more than one guest. He was interviewed as well and never mentioned anyone else."

"Well, we... uh, we never got the chance to let her know we were there. You know, what with that thing in the pool. And after what happened to Salty, I wasn't about to hang around."

"So, you didn't alert anyone in the house about the disturbance in the pool?"

"No, ma'am."

"So, your wife was inside, and you saw a maniacal killer outside, and you didn't think to let her know?" Campbell stared at him. "I find that just a little bit curious."

"I'm not proud of it," he said. "I think maybe... I guess I thought she heard us scream or something. You have no idea how goddam scary that thing in the pool was."

"I suppose not."

"Damn right."

"One last thing," said Alice, lifting yet another scrap of data from the computer. "Our crime scene folks say someone used pepper spray near the pool."

"That was me. I was tryin' to save Salty. Tryin' to get that nasty bitch to let go of my friend."

"I see. And do you always carry pepper spray with you when visiting people?"

Flynt narrowed his eyes, and his right lip twitched upward, but he remained silent.

"It's not important," Alice said. "I was just wondering."

"Screw you."

That's the best you've got? You may or may not be crazy, but you're an idiot to curse a cop. "Not exactly the response I'd hoped for. By the way, are you familiar with the term 'Person of Interest?'"

He continued to sneer. "I've heard of it."

"Well, congratulations. As of today, you are one."

His eyes widened. "What's that mean?"

"It means we're done for now," Alice said. "I need to compare notes with the on-site teams, the crime lab, and the medical examiner. That'll take some time. Meanwhile, *do not leave town* without letting me know. I'm sure I'll have more questions later."

"I didn't do anything wrong."

She shrugged. "Then you have nothing to worry about."

"So, I can go?"

"Yep."

He hurried from the room, the scent of tobacco marking his exit.

"The really weird thing about dealing with crazies," Alice reminded herself, "is that they all truly believe what they say. The hard part is figuring out which ones are right."

~*~

"His name is Abner Bowden? Good. Where does he live?" Spanos listened intently for an answer from the voice on his speaker phone. The task of locating friends of the dead man in the pool had been passed on to the same person who had done the surveillance on the Drummond estate.

The voice on the phone responded, "You mean where he *used* to live? He died last night. In the pool."

Spanos gnashed his teeth. "No, you moron! I don't care about him. I need to find the man he was with. The one who got away."

"The police have only released the name of the dead guy."

"Then you're wasting my time. Don't call me until you have something I can use." He cut the connection, wishing he could cut something from the body of the mentally defective clown he'd just been talking to.

Spanos stood and stretched. He tried to flex his arm and leg muscles but found them weak, the effort painful. The spices were killing him, sucking a little life from his body every time he used them. He didn't believe he'd become addicted to them. He could go for months without using. Indeed, the time he'd spent in prison proved that. The cravings, however, never subsided.

Where an addictive drug might hold its users in a state of euphoria, the spices made him feel the might of the gods. In the end, however, the sensations for both types of user were temporary. What Spanos desperately needed was the set of complimentary spices held by Enid Drummond, some of which had the power to heal.

Finding her had become more than an obsession; it meant life or death. Any possible connection to the whereabouts of the woman had to be investigated. That included even the most remote possibilities, like the man who'd eluded him the night before.

The memory of that night remained clear in his mind, and he had reviewed the incident at the pool several times. The man's escape had been unfortunate but not catastrophic. Finding him wouldn't take long, nor would it require a great deal of effort to extract whatever information he had. In fact, he'd thought of an interesting device to help encourage the man to talk. He'd sent an associate to pick one up at a local discount store.

Interrogations were always more fun when one could experiment with new tools and techniques.

~*~

Theo spent a good part of the day in bed. His head hurt, but he didn't know if his run-in with the monster in the pool caused it or if the bitchy cop who had given him so much lip was responsible. And as much as he wanted to forget about both of them, he couldn't. One still frightened him; the other still pissed him off.

He couldn't get his mind off the snake woman. Every time he tried to convince himself she couldn't be real, that such a vile creature couldn't possibly exist, memories of poor Salty popped into his head. His death had certainly been real.

Making matters worse, and interrupting his efforts at napping, he'd received two deliveries in the afternoon. The first notified him that Callie had filed for divorce. The second informed him a judge had issued a temporary restraining order against him. For the next thirty days, he wasn't allowed to contact Callie or go anywhere near her.

Either notice on its own would have left him seething with anger, but the combination ignited an even more intense fire.

What a scheming, ungrateful whore! What did I do to deserve this?

Though tempted to race over to her swanky mansion, break in, and rip her heart out, memories of the monster and the cop swayed him. He had to think things through first. The bitch was smarter than she looked, but then, so was he.

If anything, her asshole lawyer had gotten the restraining order. Callie wouldn't have known how to do that. He read the document again and smiled, his anger temporarily mollified. His headache even started to go away.

The order didn't say anything about her candy-ass, pepper spraying boyfriend. And though Theo didn't have the vaguest clue where the bastard lived, there was no doubt he'd be spending time with Callie at the old lady's mansion. Theo could just camp out there and keep watch. Sooner or later Callie's lover would show himself, and when he did, Theo would take him down. Hard.

~*~

Damian returned to his apartment, still trying to find some way to sort out all the insane things he'd been through the previous day. It didn't help that he'd gotten almost no sleep.

After all the food and wine, the body in the pool, the cops, and the questions, Callie had asked him to spend the night. He had agreed, and while neither of them had the energy for lovemaking, she fell asleep immediately while he lay in bed, wide awake, thinking.

Thinking! Am I a total idiot? I was lying in bed with my

arm around a beautiful woman, and all I could do was think about how the hell I ended up in that situation?

It eventually dawned on him that a woman he'd found both attractive and desirable seemed to have found the same qualities in him. That had never happened before. Working from home had many advantages, but they didn't include meeting people as friends or for developing deeper relationships. The bar scene didn't appeal to him, and he'd never been much for going to church. Online dating seemed risky, and thus he'd managed to box himself in socially. At least until he connected with Callie.

But she had serious issues, problems he would never face. If he pressed too hard now, before she had a chance to experience the freedom he knew she craved, would he scare her off?

Would it be better for their budding relationship if he didn't press his advantage? Or would she think he either didn't care or couldn't handle the fallout from her problems? How should he proceed? What should he say the next time they met?

He fell asleep at his drawing table, head down on a cartoon of a rabbit, a monkey, and a duck.

~*~

Callie thought breakfast with Damian had felt strained; neither of them wanted to deal with the events of the previous day. Damian seemed eager to leave, and she had no problem with that. Her fears from the night before no longer haunted her. At the door, as he prepared to go home, they settled for an awkward handshake rather than a kiss.

As he walked through the portico toward his car, Damian called out, "I'll give you a buzz."

"I don't have a phone," Callie said in consternation, but then she brightened. "Yet!"

"There's one in the house." He flashed his palm with a scrawl of ink on it. "I wrote the number down. Oh, and I left my number on a napkin by the toaster."

Callie waved to him as he drove away then went back inside and poured herself a cup of coffee.

Today is the first day of the rest of my life.

Though the sentiment likely came from a cheesy greeting card, it fit. Taking advantage of it, thanks to Aunt Enid, had finally become possible.

She ran through a mental list of things she needed: cell phone, computer, internet connection, clothing, maybe even a haircut. Her new job would surely require talking to people with important positions. She had to look just as professional. Her days as a timid assistant librarian were over.

I should start with the library, she thought. *Much as I hate to just quit, they'll get by without me, but I need to tell them in person. I owe it to them.*

That brought her up short. She had no way to get there, or anywhere else. She didn't think it would be possible to buy a car over the phone, especially since she had no credit history. Not knowing where else to turn, she called Gordon Parkhurst.

"I'm sorry to bother you," she said, "but I'm having a bit of a time getting started all on my own. I hoped you might be willing to give me some advice."

"Of course," he said. "I'd be happy to, even if your Aunt Enid hadn't given me explicit instructions to help you in any way I can."

"She did?"

"Absolutely."

"*Recently?*"

"As a matter of fact, yes. Now, what do you need help with?"

Callie eased back and relaxed; there was hope. *Aunt Enid really is alive.* "I have a ton of things to do and places to go. I think I need a car."

"That shouldn't be a problem," Parkhurst said. "But I'm surprised you didn't like the one we left for you in the garage."

"You... What?" She hadn't even looked in the garage. Surely they hadn't....

"It's not new, but it's got low mileage, and it's still under warranty. I drove it myself to make sure it operated properly and had all the appropriate accessories."

Stunned, Callie had no idea what to say.

"Ms. Flynt?" He sounded concerned.

"Yes!"

"Just so you know, we advised your husband, in writing, that you're seeking a no-fault divorce. The papers were delivered yesterday along with notice that a restraining order is now in force. If he's smart, he'll stay away from you. That, however, remains to be seen, so I urge you to stay alert. Based on what little I've seen of your husband, I wouldn't trust him to act in accordance with the order."

"Nor would I," she said. "Maybe I should get a guard dog."

"It's worth considering, but I suggest you get settled in your new role before you make any moves like that. You may be traveling a great deal. My advice would be to live your new life for a while, enjoy it. Just remember one thing." He paused.

Callie waited for him to continue. "One thing?"

"Mrs. Drummond wanted me to be sure you understood the job she's providing you is for *your* benefit, not Mr. Flynt's. She didn't insist that you get a divorce. That, she believed, would not have been reasonable if you wished to remain with him. If that turned out to be the case, she instructed me to rescind the job offer and any benefits which derived from it: the house, the car, the expense account, etc. The funds from your trust, however, would continue no matter what you decide."

"Oh."

"Do you understand and accept these terms?"

"Yes." *If only all my decisions were so easy!*

"The car keys are in the glove box."

"This is all so... amazing!"

"Have you done much driving lately?"

She wondered briefly if her driver's license had expired. She hadn't used it for more than identification since her marriage. "Driving? Lately? Almost none. Theo always said– Y'know what? The hell with Theo."

Parkhurst's smile somehow came through his voice on the phone. "I suggest you practice a bit on the side streets before you venture very far out."

"What about insurance and–"

"All taken care of. Now, I hate to end this conversation, but I have another client waiting. Take some time; get used to the car; buy yourself a new wardrobe. Get anything you need. And most importantly, if you need help, call me."

"You're a lifesaver," Callie said. "I don't know how to thank you."

"You don't have to. It's a pleasure," he said. "But don't forget, it's your Aunt Enid who's making all this possible."

She hung up the phone and raced to the garage where she found a dark green, BMW convertible sitting in the middle of the three spaces. The car door opened quietly, and she slid behind the wheel relishing the cool feel of the leather seat. She found the keys right where Parkhurst said they would be. The engine cranked at the touch of a button.

The sound only served to make her new-found freedom more evident, as if the tears on her cheeks weren't enough.

~*~

Julianne, the masseuse working on Spanos, asked repeatedly if the techniques she applied caused him any pain.

"Just shut up and work. Quietly. You'll know if you hurt me."

That seemed to do the trick, but the stupidity level among some of his employees still irked him. Fortunately, finding replacements had not proven difficult. Finding one as attractive as Julianne, who would also perform the additional services he required, would not be so easy.

When the phone rang he pressed the speaker button. "What?" Few things justified interrupting a massage.

"I think I've spotted the man you're looking for."

Spanos waved Julianne away. "Where?"

"He returned to the Drummond place. He's nesting in the woods and apparently doing his own surveillance."

Could it be true? "Is he still there?"

"Yes sir."

"Then," Spanos growled, "why haven't you grabbed him?"

"Men are on their way now, sir. Where would you like him delivered?"

"Bring him here, and only use as much force as necessary. I'll be waiting in the basement lounge."

"You have a lounge in your basement?" Julianne asked as she removed what little clothing she had on.

Spanos responded with a humorless laugh. "Oh, yes. Indeed."

"Would you rather we finish down there?"

He flopped his head into the open space on the massage table reserved for a patron's face. "You wouldn't like it down there," he said. "You wouldn't like it at all."

As he relaxed under the woman's ministrations, Spanos debated whether to help himself to a bit of spice. Since he could no longer rely on his own physical responses, his thoughts drifted toward Priapus, whom he considered the god of erections. The spice, however, in addition to debilitating him further, might leave him supernaturally aroused for much longer than necessary.

Decisions, decisions.

~*~

While never a boy scout or a fan of camping trips, Theo knew enough to prepare for the sorts of things one always found in the woods: spiders, ticks, and mosquitoes. He felt reasonably sure he could spot poison ivy, but poison oak was another matter. Therefore, he avoided anything that looked like it might make him even more miserable.

Into the woods he'd dragged a sleeping bag, a cooler, and a lightweight slingback chair which Big Lou called a "backpacker's dream." It wasn't too bad, Theo thought as he opened another beer. Though determined to catch Callie's boyfriend and thoroughly whip his ass, Theo hadn't given much thought to how boring it would be waiting for him to show up at the mansion. He wished he'd brought something along to pass the time, like a handful of Big Lou's nudie magazines. He even had one that featured some of the wrestling divas.

As he daydreamed about being a photographer and working with naked females, he failed to notice the approach of two armed men until they burst into his makeshift campsite.

"Shut up and don't move," growled one as they flanked him with guns drawn.

Theo's head wrenched from side to side. "What the hell? Who–"

"You're coming with us."

"The fuck I am!"

The second man struck so fast Theo didn't see the blow coming. He simply felt a sudden sharp pain in his head and tasted dirt and pine needles in his mouth.

Pressing up off the forest floor, he asked, "Did-- Did *Callie* send you?"

"Put your hands behind your back."

Theo complied, and as soon as they secured his wrists, they slipped a cloth bag over his head, blinding him except for a slivered opening that allowed him to see his feet.

As they dragged him to a van and shoved him in the back, Theo shouted, "Who the hell are you? And where are you taking me?"

Neither man answered him.

As the van began to move, Theo shifted on the floor in an effort to get comfortable.

He didn't succeed.

Chapter Eight

"The gods, too, are fond of a joke." —Aristotle

Callie drove to the library before beginning her errands. After profuse apologies to the head librarian for her sudden resignation, she made her way to the bank of computers available to patrons.

Despite everything which had happened in such a short span of time, Callie never forgot how quickly Theo healed after being beaten. The only thing that could have accounted for it was the sprinkling of spice she added to their food. The fact her own bruises had cleared up in record time seemed to confirm it.

She felt a slight twinge of guilt for smiling about how thoroughly the alleged attackers had pummeled him. Though he would never acknowledge it, he was way past due for a taste of his own medicine.

Bon appétit, you big jerk.

Forcing herself back on track, she used the computer to generate a selection of books on Greek gods and goddesses. If the rest of the little jars Aunt Enid left her contained the essence of those ancient deities, she needed to know a great deal more about them.

She found a half dozen books which looked promising and hoped she'd find time to read them. Having to choose between miracles had never entered her mind, and yet that's what she now faced—the wonder of freedom and the phenomenon of Enid's spices.

Neither could be ignored.

She checked out her books, waved goodbye to the Head Librarian, and went in search of the nearest store carrying clothing suitable for a young woman working in a responsible, professional role. Her mind bursting with ideas, she had no interest in worrying about Theo or anything else.

It was finally time to get on with her life.

~*~

Theo's mind raced from one fear to another. He'd seen enough movies to know the depth of his predicament. The scenario he'd just endured—being bound and thrown in a van, then driven to an unknown location by people he didn't know—touched on more than one film scene that ended badly for the person kidnaped.

All too soon the ride ended. Two men, presumably the same ones who grabbed him outside the old lady's house, dragged him into a building and hauled him down a flight of stairs.

"I can walk. Lemme walk," he said, trying not to wail.

They answered him with a quick jab to his ribs. He would have dropped to the floor if they hadn't been holding his arms.

The bag came off his head only after he'd been securely tied to an unpadded armchair. The two men then stepped to the rear of the room where he could no longer see them.

"Can you at least tell me what you want? This is crazy. I'm not rich, but you can have anything I own, just please let me go."

"Be quiet," one of them said. "You'll find out everything you need to know when Mr. Spanos arrives."

"Who is–"

A vile-tasting cloth suddenly filled his mouth and cut off his words. Tempted to struggle, he remembered the blow to his head he'd received earlier and abandoned any thoughts of resistance.

The wait might have lasted minutes or hours. Theo's imagination fueled his dread, and every second lasted an eternity. By turning his head from side to side, he could see most of the room except for the stairs located in the portion immediately behind him. There wasn't much to see.

An easy chair occupied the space directly across from him while shelves adorned plain block walls all around. Harsh light flooded down from an overhead fluorescent fixture that flickered and buzzed on a regular basis providing irritants in addition to his fear.

At long last he heard steps on the stairs and movement just out of sight. He held his breath and waited as a trickle of sweat dripped from his temple to the collar of his T-shirt.

An older, heavy set man stepped in front of him as he poked about in Theo's wallet. His skin had a mottled, saggy look, and his thinning hair appeared a sickly shade of yellow.

At a gesture from the old man, the towel was yanked from Theo's mouth. He worked his jaw once it became free. He wanted to say something, but his throat had gone too dry to form words.

The old man held his driver's license up to the light and read from it. "Theodore Flynt."

Theo nodded.

"You're undoubtedly wondering why I had you brought here."

Theo nodded again, still not prepared to speak.

"We met the other night," he said. "I'm Aristotle Spanos."

Theo stared at him, desperately trying to remember ever having seen the man before. *At Toni's? At the union hall?* "I don't– Uh, I can't–"

"I was in the pool at Enid Drummond's house. Your companion was in the water with me." He licked his lips in an overly dramatic fashion. "Tasty fellow. It's a pity I didn't have time to finish him; I was busy chasing you."

Theo's heartrate redlined, and his words slammed into each other. "But you– It was a woman– You can't– Oh, Christ! What are you saying? How?"

"Never mind how, Mr. Flynt. That's my little secret. Just know that at any time I choose, I can become the most fearsome of creatures. The beast you encountered in the pool is but one of many."

He paused and walked to one of the shelves behind the easy chair. There he retrieved something which he held behind his back. With a gesture of his free hand, one of the silent men produced an orange extension cord which he plugged into an outlet. He handed the other end to Spanos who brought forth the electric charcoal starter he'd been hiding behind his back. The looped end had not yet begun to glow, but when Spanos plugged it in, Theo knew it soon would.

"Do you remember the question I asked you that night?" Spanos asked.

Theo's mind whirled. "I think so." *God, I hope so!*

Spanos pointed the charcoal starter at him. "Care to answer it now?"

"I– Uh– You want to know where my wife's aunt is?"

The heavy brows above the old man's eyes dipped sharply down. "Your wife's *aunt?*"

"Yeah. Enid Drummond. She owns the house where–"

"Yes, yes, I know all that. But I didn't know she had living relatives. Where is Enid Drummond?"

"Greece, I think," Theo said, eager to please. "Assuming she's still alive."

The old man stared at him, his jaws tight. "What makes you think she isn't?"

"Shit, man. We haven't heard from her in years. She's really old, older than you even." He instantly regretted his words, but Spanos didn't seem to care.

"So, your wife knows where she is?"

Theo shook his head vigorously. "No. She's as much in the dark as I am. Unless…."

The charcoal starter began to glow, and the old man moved closer. "Unless what?"

"She's got a lawyer. Parker or Packer, something like that. I think he stays in touch with her, Callie's aunt I mean." He couldn't keep his lip from trembling. "Please don't hurt me. I'll tell you everything I know. Just don't–"

"Silence," hissed Spanos. "Does this attorney live here in Atlanta?"

"Yes! Yes, he does. I'm sure of it."

"And the name again?"

Theo swallowed, wishing he'd taken the time to write it down. Then he remembered the letterhead on the divorce notice. "It's Parkhurst. Yeah. I'm sure of it. Gordon, I think. Gordon Parkhurst."

Spanos handed the charcoal starter to one of his men who carried it out of sight behind Theo. "What were you doing at the house?"

"Just trying to get to my wife. She's been hanging with some asshole who–"

The old man held up his hand, palm out. "Do you think I care about your pathetic problems?"

"I, uh, guess not," Theo said.

"You have, however, been quite helpful." Spanos gestured once again to his men. "So, you've earned my gratitude." He waited for one of the men to hand him a gun. "And a quick death."

"Wait!" screamed Theo. "Stop!"

"Why?" Clearly bored, Spanos said, "You're wasting my time."

Theo struggled to find a bargaining chip. "If– If you want something the old lady has, you could be looking in the wrong place."

The old man showed some interest. "What do you mean?"

"You said you changed into that– that thing in the pool. Well, Callie did something sorta like that to me."

Spanos' eyes narrowed into slits. "Go on."

"She put something in my dinner, some funny tasting stuff. It did something, made me heal up overnight."

"So?"

"You don't understand. I got beat up by four or five guys, Mexican gangbangers. I was nearly dead, bleedin' all over, but the next day I was fine. No cuts, no bruises. Nothin'. I felt great. Maybe she's already got whatever it is you want from her aunt."

Spanos rubbed his chin.

"I know where she goes," Theo said. "I can find her for you. Please, lemme help."

~*~

Damian spent the morning fighting sleep and alternately cursing himself for lacking imagination and for the inability to get Callie out of his mind. Nothing seemed to be working right, personally or professionally.

The very fact he couldn't free himself from thoughts of the woman—her gentle manner, her laugh, her smile, and a dozen other things—seemed to indicate that, at the very least, infatuation had set in.

Was it love? Could it be love? I barely know her.

He definitely cared about her and remained angry at the idiot she married. And what about that? How could she not have seen what an asshole he is? It made no sense. On the other hand, maybe *she* had once been infatuated with him. So much so that she couldn't see his faults, as obvious as they were to everyone else.

Have I fallen into a similar predicament? Lord knows, the girl has some baggage. And yet....

Staring at the unfinished illustration on his drawing board didn't help. The rabbit looked way too much like Callie, and the monkey had become a hairy version of her husband. He erased the rough, pencil sketch of the duck before it evolved any further into a self-portrait and wiped the picture free of leftover rubbings.

Muttering obscenities he rarely used when working, Damian pushed himself away from the work station. Too conflicted to go on, he committed himself to a quick library visit. With any luck he might catch Callie there, though he suspected she had more important things on her mind.

A goddamn duck? Really?

He grabbed his keys and drove to the library. As if his day weren't already going badly, he nearly ran over a little dog when he parked the car. He called to it, thinking how fun it might be to base a cartoon on the small, white mutt with black spots. At the last moment, however, it turned and walked away.

~*~

All too aware of the debilitating aftereffects of the spices, Spanos knew he could no longer use them unless conditions became so dire he had no other choice. That didn't mean he couldn't allow surrogates to use them for his purposes. So long as they understood their survival depended upon following his strict orders, they would do his bidding as instructed.

Theodore Flynt presented just such an opportunity. Spanos recognized his type; he'd seen it often enough in and out of prison—a weak-willed man, streetwise but easily manipulated.

Lowering his gun hand to his side, Spanos said, "You claim you're willing to help me. Does that mean you'd sacrifice your wife to save yourself?"

"That's a shitty way to put it."

"Perhaps you can put it in a better light."

Theo shifted in the chair. "It's a case of just desserts. She's dumping me so she won't have to share her inheritance. If she's dies before the divorce, I get it all."

"You understand," Spanos said, "I *don't* want her killed. At least, not until she's told me everything I want to know."

"Yeah, yeah. Of course. I get that."

"So you'll grab her and bring her to me?"

"Sure. Just tell me where and when."

Spanos regarded him with suspicion. "What if you're recognized?"

"I'll wear a mask or something."

"Are you familiar with DNA?" Spanos asked, though he'd already guessed the answer.

"They talk about it on TV. It's kinda like fingerprints. So, I guess I'd need to wear gloves, too."

"I have a better solution," Spanos said. "I can provide a disguise so unique your own mother wouldn't recognize you. And here's the best part: when you're done, all traces of it will disappear. You needn't worry about fingerprints, DNA, security camera footage or anything else."

Theo looked uncertain. "What if someone tries to stop me?"

"I can't imagine anyone would. Your appearance will

most likely scare them away."

"My appearance?"

"Your disguise."

"Oh, right." He looked down at the gun in Spanos' hand. "You don't need that."

"I'll hold on to it in case you screw things up. In that case, it won't matter if you're recognized. You'll be quite dead, and no one will be able to connect you to me."

Theo drew back as far as the chair would allow. "I'll do it. Any way you want. The disguise thing is fine. Just tell me what to do."

"Good," Spanos said. "We'll get started this afternoon."

~*~

Never in her life had Callie spent so much money on clothing, or bought so many different things. She needed everything, not just a few outfits that matched her new status. Fortunately, the shopkeeper produced just what she needed, from undergarments to outerwear and everything in between.

Callie worried she might not fit everything in her car and said as much.

The shopkeeper waved off the objection. "I can have it delivered. You can go on about your business; I'll take care of everything."

"Clothing stores deliver?" The idea had never crossed Callie's mind.

The shopkeeper pointed at the merchandise they had assembled. "I'll be happy to pay a driver to make the delivery. And if no one's available, I'll bring it by your house myself."

"You'd *do* that?"

"To keep a brand new customer like you happy? Of course!"

Callie slipped into one of her new outfits while the shopkeeper packed up the rest of her clothes.

"I left my old things in the changing room," Callie said.

"Would you like me to send them along with everything else?"

On the brink of agreeing, Callie changed her mind. "No. I don't want them anymore. They're a part of my past. You can toss them or give them away; I don't care. I'm not that person anymore."

She used the store's phone to call Gordon Parkhurst hoping to get in to see him without an appointment.

"I already have a number of meetings set up for this afternoon," he said, "But I should have some free time in the morning."

"Then I'll come by first thing."

"If you'll give me your cell phone number, I'll be able to call you if something comes up."

"Oh," Callie said. "I don't have one yet. But I'm going to take care of that this afternoon. I'll call and leave my number with your secretary."

"Excellent. See you in the morning!"

"Next up," Callie told herself, "pick out a phone. Even if you only have two numbers to put in it."

~*~

The two thugs who worked for Spanos drove Theo to the library that afternoon. Theo sat in back, growing increasingly more nervous about what he had agreed to do. Spanos had given him nothing in the way of a costume or a disguise. He still wore the same University of Alabama T-shirt and jeans he'd been wearing in the woods when the two hoods grabbed him earlier that day.

"The old man said he'd give me a disguise," Theo said, trying not to whine.

"We got it right here," said the bald one from his seat beside the redheaded driver. "Just hang on a bit, and we'll give it to you."

"Where'm I gonna change?"

"In the car, dumb ass. Where did you think?"

He and the driver found that idea uproariously funny. Theo became suspicious but kept quiet, content to wait and see what happened next.

Finding a shady spot at the far end of the library lot, the driver pulled in and parked. "We'll wait here for you to come out with the woman."

"And here's your disguise," said the bald thug riding shotgun. He handed Theo a little envelope and a travel mug.

"What the hell kinda disguise is this?" Theo asked, flummoxed.

"Take the cap off the mug and sprinkle in the powder. You can stir it with your finger."

Shit! They're gonna poison me.

"What's it supposed to do?"

"You'll see."

"Please," Theo said. "I don't wanna die. I'm not gonna drink poison."

The driver pulled out a gun and aimed it at Theo's head. "It's not like you've got a choice. Put the powder in the water, stir it up, and drink it. We don't have all day."

His hands shook so badly he spilled some of the water before he could add the powder.

"Will you get on with it for cryin' out loud! It won't kill ya, I promise," said the driver.

"Gimme that shit," said the other thug. "I'll mix it up for ya. While I'm doing that, you need to take your pants off."

"What for?"

"Just do it. You'll thank me later." He handed the mug to Theo and mimed for him to drink up.

Theo stared at the concoction then sniffed it but couldn't detect a scent.

"Just drink it!" growled the driver, still waving the gun at him.

Theo tasted the liquid. The bitterness assaulted him instantly, and he pulled the container away from his mouth. "This tastes like shit."

"Not my problem," said the driver. "Drink up."

Theo took another breath, closed his eyes, and drank the contents of the cup in two huge gulps.

"There now, that wasn't so bad, was it?" asked the bald guy riding shotgun.

Anticipating an agonizing death, Theo sat back in the seat and closed his eyes. He could feel something gurgling in his stomach as the nerves throughout his body began to tingle.

"Got those pants off?"

"What? No."

"Get to it then. You're gonna pass out pretty soon, and I don't wanna do it for you."

The drowsiness came on quickly, but Theo did as he was told.

The driver put his gun away. "You wearin' boxers or briefs?"

"What the hell kinda question is that?"

The thug shook his head. "I'm tryin' to save you some grief is all."

"Boxers," Theo said.

"Good."

His eyelids had grown too heavy to keep open.

Oh God, I'm gonna die.

It was his last thought before losing consciousness.

~*~

Damian's first stop had been the Head Librarian's office to inquire about Callie.

"She came in this morning and quit her job," the woman said. "I have no idea why. Is there something I can help you with?"

"No. Thanks anyway," Damian said, unable to hide the disappointment in his voice.

He heard a child's laughter from the far side of the library, undoubtedly from the children's section. On a whim, he headed that way. "Might as well check out the competition," he told himself. "Maybe I'll get a better fix on how the stupid duck should look. And the monkey, too."

He worked his way through a number of newly

released books without finding anything useful. His search had been interrupted several times by the excited reactions of a number of very young readers. He wished he could capture their exuberance and pour it into his illustrations. At least for the one that kept reminding him of Callie.

A shout of outrage from the front of the building shattered the library's collective calm. Everyone stopped what they were doing to see what caused it.

Damian stared past a handful of equally curious library patrons at a short man who had just entered the building and likely elicited the scream. Because of the desks and tables in the way, Damian could only see him from the chest up. He did not relish the view.

Extremely short and bearing a visage likely to make children run away in fear, still it was something else about the man that had caused the original exclamation. Damian doubted it had anything to do with his filthy, Roll Tide T-shirt. He walked closer for a better look.

And instantly regretted it.

The little man wore no pants and sported the penis of a Percheron which poked out from the center of his boxer shorts. Easily as long as his arm, the erect member bobbed as he walked and protruded like some sort of bizarre divining rod.

"Where the hell is Callie Flynt?" he yelled as he stalked around the central area, his movements hampered by the enormous erection. He stopped behind the check-out counter where he grabbed a large pair of scissors from a drawer.

The Head Librarian bustled forth from her office and came to an abrupt and incredulous halt when she saw him. It took her a moment to collect her wits. "What do you think you're doing coming in here like that?"

"Like what?" he asked, waving his engorged phallus like a firehose. "Where's Callie?"

"She quit," Damian said, coming to the librarian's side. "Who wants to know?"

The grotesque little Bama fan thumbed his chest. "Me." He then squinted at Damian, his brows furrowing. "I know you."

"I doubt that," Damian said. "Why don't you get out of here before we call the police?"

The librarian whipped out a cell phone and made a show of dialing. "I'll have them on the line any moment."

"I ain't leavin' alone," said the troll-like figure. After a quick look around, he hurried toward the children's section leaving a wake of astonished patrons behind. Damian hurried after him, determined not to let him harm anyone.

The intruder beat him to the destination and grabbed a tow-headed boy from the arms of his mother. Screaming at him while struggling to hang on to an even younger child, the woman pleaded for help.

Damian blocked the little man's exit. "Put the boy down," he commanded.

"No." The child's sobs only grew louder when the point of one scissor blade was pressed into his throat. "Get outta my way," growled the short, ugly cretin.

Damian briefly considered mounting some sort of attack, but he had nothing handy save children's books and kindergarten furniture. "Put him down. Take me instead," he offered. "I won't resist."

The gnomish intruder considered his words. "You'll come along quietly?"

"Yeah."

"I'll stab the shit outta you if you don't."

The scissors looked far more menacing than Damian would have thought possible. "Sure. No problem. There's no need to hurt anybody."

"The police are on their way," shouted the librarian.

"Move!" yelled the man with the monstrous appendage as he released the child and jabbed the scissors at Damian's crotch.

Damian walked ahead of him, moving fast enough to stay out of range of the little man's makeshift weapon. As they left the building, Damian followed a command to proceed to the back of the parking lot where two men stood beside a dark sedan.

When they reached the car, the larger of the two, a redhead, looked from Damian to the man who'd captured him. "Where's the woman, and who the hell is this?"

"She wasn't in there," the little man said.

"Did you search the place?"

"I'm tellin' ya, she wasn't in there. I grabbed this asshole instead." He waved the scissors at Damian.

"Mr. Spanos isn't interested in anyone else."

"He probably knows where she is!"

Damian feigned surprise. "Where who is? I have no idea what he's talking about."

"He's lying!" yelled the dwarf, still in a tumescent state. The features on his face coalesced into a dark sneer as he drew his hand back to stab Damian with the scissors.

The redhead put a restraining hand on him. "Chill out.

I'll take care of this." He then whirled around and landed a vicious, roundhouse punch that drove Damian to the pavement.

He lay on the hot asphalt surface, dazed and disoriented. A police siren wailed in the distance, and the car beside him drove away, but paying attention to anything proved impossible until something began licking his face.

He looked up into the eyes of the little white dog he'd nearly run over. A big black spot covered one eye as he put a paw on Damian's chest and continued to lick him.

Damian managed to sit up, and the dog stood guard in front of him as a police car pulled up alongside them.

"You okay?" the officer asked.

Damian rubbed his jaw with one hand and petted the dog with the other. "I think so." He shook his head to clear it, thankful that nothing rattled around inside. "They're gone now."

"They? We heard there was only one."

"Just one in the library, but two more were out here in a car waiting for him."

The cop appeared sympathetic. "Did you recognize them?"

"No," said Damian, "but I can damned sure draw you a good likeness of them."

Chapter Nine

"The gods plant reason in mankind, of all good gifts the highest." —Sophocles

Detective Alice Campbell looked at the three sketches in front of her. Two had significant detail and could have passed for something posed or drawn from a photo. The third image failed in most respects. She tapped it with a fingernail.

"I'm sorry about that one," said the man in front of her. "I didn't pay much attention to him. He never said much. He might have just been along for the ride. What I distinctly remember was the guy with red hair who decked me."

Alice made a note, then returned to the first drawing and shuddered. It wasn't the first time and likely wouldn't be the last.

"Don't get me wrong, Mr. Dean. We certainly appreciate your help in this matter, and these sketches are... remarkable, especially of the man who entered the library. But don't you think you've exaggerated his...

uhm... genitalia just a bit?"

Damian Dean shook his head. "Sadly, no. If anything, I might have made them–*it*–look smaller than it was."

Alice scratched her head. After all these years she still hadn't gotten used to talking to the crazies, people whose stories could not possibly be true. This time, however, the man's drawings confirmed what several other observers swore they'd seen. "And you talked to him?"

"Yes. And talked him out of kidnapping a child."

"By offering yourself, I understand," she said. "A risky thing to do."

"I thought I'd have a better chance against him than a toddler would."

She looked once again at the half naked lunatic in the drawing. "Can't say this does much for the Alabama brand."

"I seriously doubt the University put him up to it," Damian said.

"No, I'm sure they didn't." She set the drawing aside. "Earlier you said he asked about someone named Callie. I don't suppose you know her."

"She's a friend," he said. "We met at the library, but she no longer works there."

"Do you know how to reach her?"

He looked up the phone number of her aunt's estate and recited it. Alice read it back to make sure she had it right. "I'll contact her later," she said. "In case she knows something that'll help."

"Assuming you find this—pardon my language—prick, what'll you charge him with?"

"Other than indecent exposure and disturbing the peace?"

"Yeah."

"Based on what we've heard from you and others who were in the library, an assault charge is most likely. The scissors could easily be considered a lethal weapon. And then there's the attempted kidnapping of the child."

"Not to mention what his buddy did to me," Damian said. "My jaw still aches. I'd be all too happy to testify against them."

"Did you note what kind of car they drove?"

"Sorry. Didn't pay much attention. It was gray, boring. Pretty much like every other gray car on the road."

"If you think of anything else, please give me a call." She handed him a business card as she rose to her feet. "We'll be in touch when the time comes. Do you mind if I keep these drawings?"

"Not at all. I have the originals if you need them."

"Thank you for your time, Mr. Dean."

She watched him depart then sat back down at her desk, her mind embroiled by the inexplicable image of a munchkin with a pointlessly huge member. What was next? First a flesh-eating, half-woman/half-snake monster, and now this. What was the world coming to?

While thinking of the anatomical absurdity on the freak who invaded the library, the term "priapism" came to mind. Not certain she had the definition precisely right, she looked it up. In short order she learned more than she ever wanted to know, including the condition's namesake, the Greek god Priapus.

On a whim, she looked up some other Greek gods and found one that matched the description of the creature supposedly sighted in the swimming pool: Echidna.

I'll be damned.

On a hunch, she logged back into the archive of APD detective notes and began looking for unsolved crimes involving unusual creatures.

~*~

"I knew I shouldn't have trusted you," Spanos snarled the next day when he had Theo trotted out to account for his failed mission at the library. "Where's my damned gun?"

"It's not my fault she wasn't there!" Theo wailed. "How was I s'posed to know she quit? C'mon, gimme another chance."

"What's more," Spanos said as he accepted a 9MM automatic from the redheaded thug, "I can't believe I wasted any of my precious spice on you."

Theo hadn't quite gotten over the incident. "I would've been a helluva lot better off without it. I can't believe how big my damn–"

Spanos stared at him. "How could I have listened to such a complete and utter moron?" He checked to be sure the weapon was loaded. "Someone, please, tell me why I shouldn't just shoot–"

"I can get Parkhurst for you!" Theo said, pleading. "I know I can. He'll tell you where to find Callie's aunt. He knows. I'm sure of it."

Spanos drummed his fingers on his desk as he considered the possibilities. At length he broke into an odd smile. "Are you familiar with the name, Polyphemus?"

"Polly who?" Theo doubted he'd ever met anyone named Polly. At least not since grade school.

"I thought not." Spanos sat back and continued to smile. After putting his palms together, he tapped his fingertips in sequence. "I think it might be fun to let you and Polyphemus interrogate this attorney friend of yours."

"I never said Parkhurst was a fr–"

"Shut up and listen!" Spanos barked, thrusting himself forward in his chair. "I'm going to tell you exactly what you're going to do. And this time, don't you dare screw it up."

~*~

Callie smiled as she entered Gordon Parkhurst's office. She liked the man, a feeling that undoubtedly evolved from Theo's disdain for him. "Thank you for seeing me."

He waved her in. "Coffee? Help yourself." He swept his arm toward a well-stocked beverage service on a nearby table. "Now, how can I be of service?"

Callie discussed her feelings about the job her aunt had arranged for her. "I've never had so much responsibility. I'm afraid I'll mess things up, and I don't want to disappoint Aunt Enid."

"You won't," Parkhurst assured her. "Enid's a great judge of character, and if she thinks you can do it, then you can."

"It's not as easy as that." Callie frowned. "I can dress for the part, but when it comes right down to it, I don't know where to begin. I have no idea who to talk to or what to say."

Parkhurst opened a drawer in his desk and extracted a file folder. "I confess, I've once again taken a few liberties. But all of them were on your behalf. I hope you won't mind."

She couldn't help but be a bit suspicious. "What kind of liberties?"

"I sent letters to a number of institutions I thought might have the space and the sort of interest required to house and promote Enid's collection of religious artifacts."

Callie's anxiety began to fade. "Have any responded?"

"Quite a few," he said proudly. "I thought doing it this way would save you some time and effort. When you're ready, you can make arrangements to visit these places and discuss the possibility of their becoming a host. If you find more than one potential location, there's always the option of making this a travelling exhibit."

"That would be wonderful," Callie said, feeling better about everything.

"You'll need to produce something of a catalog," he said. "It wouldn't be wise to transport more than one or two of the actual artifacts for examination. But, they'll need to see something to assure themselves of the collection's quality and authenticity."

"She wouldn't exaggerate such things, would she?"

Parkhurst chuckled. "She wouldn't have to. It's been a long, long time, but I can still recall when she showed me some of the items she'd pulled together. I quite fancied Thor's drinking cup." He shook his head. "It's exquisite. But Enid also showed me some items she originally thought were genuine, but which she ultimately determined were fakes. Her goal was to find what she called 'god-related artifacts,' things people actually believed in. Just because something looked old or mysterious didn't mean it met her criteria."

Callie sat back with her hands in her lap. "I'm a little surprised she didn't try to sell them to someone."

"She certainly doesn't need the money," the attorney said. "She wanted to share what she'd discovered, but she didn't want to invite the world to her home. Nor did she care to establish a museum of her own. The collection isn't that large. She's told me on more than one occasion she has no interest in creating what she called 'just another roadside attraction.'"

"So, how many places will I need to investigate?" Callie asked.

"That depends on how diligent you are." He opened the file folder and fanned out a sheaf of correspondence. "At least thirty institutions have responded positively thus far. There could be more."

Callie felt her eyes widen. "Thirty?"

"It's a unique collection and extraordinarily well documented. It's going to take a while to locate the best possible site, or sites, for a display."

"I need to get busy," Callie said.

Parkhurst handed her the folder. "Indeed you do."

~*~

Spanos had his driver park in a spot that afforded him a good view of the office building's parking lot. When Theo came out, hopefully in the company of Enid Drummond's attorney, Spanos could observe everything without having to leave the air conditioned comfort of his vehicle.

And if Enid's incompetent nephew-in-law failed to follow his orders, Spanos and his henchmen would be close enough to take over.

As the lunch hour began, a stream of people left the building. Theo and the attorney strolled out in the midst of them. No one seemed to notice that Theo kept the muzzle of his empty weapon pressed against Parkhurst's side. Theo knew the gun was useless; Parkhurst didn't. Their clothing kept the gun hidden well enough. Spanos smiled. Everything appeared to be going according to plan.

He watched as Theo accompanied Parkhurst to the car Spanos had given him, a non-descript Ford sedan in need of a wash and a good deal of touch-up paint. His driver had stolen it earlier that day. Theo dutifully waited until no one else was in sight, then secured Parkhurst's phone, opened the trunk, and forced him to crawl in.

Spanos felt a momentary twinge of regret as the aging barrister slowly, and with difficulty, complied with the younger man's demands. When he finally managed to compress himself into the available space, Theo shut the lid as he had been instructed.

With a slight wiggle of anticipation, Spanos concentrated on the scene; the best part would follow very soon.

"Pull a little closer," he told the driver. "I don't want to miss anything."

Clearly visible sitting behind the wheel, Theo continued following his instructions. He opened the same travel mug he'd used at the library, emptied into it the powdered contents of the envelope Spanos had given him, stirred it with his finger, and drank it all down. He then lowered all the windows.

Spanos held his breath; the transformation would soon begin.

Theo appeared drowsy, and he sat back, his skull against the headrest.

Breathing again, Spanos checked his watch.

What was taking so long? Come on, come on!

He rolled down his own window, sacrificing a bit of air-conditioned comfort in order to improve his hearing.

Thumping.

A muffled yell.

An unhappy Parkhurst clearly wanted out. His pounding on the trunk lid from inside had become rhythmic. Spanos could only imagine how hot and uncomfortable he had to be and wondered briefly if he could have gotten into the tight space as the lawyer had. He doubted it. The spice had left him fat and far too fragile.

What the hell was going on? Why hadn't Theo's transformation begun? Was the wrong spice in the envelope?

No, he decided, that wasn't possible. There had been no mix-up; he simply needed to be more patient.

And as expected, Theo's body finally began to expand.

Spanos tapped his driver on the shoulder. "Go, now. Get the lawyer's phone, then come back here. Hurry!"

As the redhead raced toward the Toyota, Spanos grinned. He'd never tried the cyclopean spice himself. The mere thought of doing so inspired nightmares. Theo would provide him with all the knowledge he needed, whether he survived or not.

After a quick search, the driver grabbed Theo's gun and the lawyer's phone from the front seat of the Ford and returned. He handed them to Spanos and resumed his spot behind the wheel.

Satisfied with events thus far, Spanos concentrated on the scene inside the stolen car. The swelling continued, stretching Theo's Roll Tide T-shirt to the limit. When it burst, his expanding flesh looked like soft dough suddenly uncompressed from a tube of Brown 'N Serve rolls. In this case, however, the "dough" continued to rise. Soon, Theo's still-growing body filled the front interior of the car.

Though Parkhurst continued his futile attempts to gain attention, the sounds emanating from the passenger compartment grew in volume. When Theo's body completely outgrew the front seat area, the backs of the seats gave way with a grinding sound. Theo swelled into the rear seat area.

A large yet still-expanding foot protruded from a front window; an arm popped out from a window in the back. Though the entire passenger compartment was all but completely full, the expansion went on.

Spanos remained riveted, unable to stop watching. "Are you filming this?" he asked the driver.

"I– Uh. Hang on, I'll–"

"Never mind, you idiot. It's too late. It's almost over."

The rear window shattered under the pressure from inside, sending a cascade of small, angular glass fragments flowing across the trunk lid. For a brief span, Parkhurst quit pounding.

The windshield popped free of its frame followed by what looked like part of the monster's one-eyed face.

More flesh flowed through all the windows, but the steel frame of the car didn't give. Blood spurted from a hundred places as Theo's distended skin ruptured under the stress.

Eventually, the process ended. Theo never woke up. At least, not in time to scream.

And that's a pity.

"Shouldn't we go now, boss?" The driver asked.

"Not yet," Spanos said. He had never been quite sure the process would go in reverse if the subject died while in the guise of a host spice. It seemed logical, but he'd been hesitant to use up the precious powder just to find out, and he certainly wasn't about to experiment on himself.

Fortunately, the reverse transformation process began before too many of the office workers returned from lunch. Spanos had the driver park immediately behind the wretched Ford to block the view of the car which bore thick smears of blood on all sides.

When too many workers returning from lunch spotted the bloody car, Spanos told the driver to get moving. He had no intention of being in the vicinity when the police arrived.

As they pulled out of the parking lot, Spanos eased back in his seat, examined the lawyer's phone in his hand, and relaxed. Thus far, everything had proceeded according to plan.

~*~

The little white dog with black spots stared up at Damian as if the two were long lost siblings. "Dogs can't smile, y'know," he told the pooch. "Except maybe in cartoons."

With a slight tilt of his head, the dog seemed to indicate he was listening, if not exactly comprehending.

"I can't take you home with me," Damian told him after spending the better part of two hours trying to figure out to whom the dog belonged. The dog had no collar, and not a soul stepped forward with usable information.

And yet, he didn't appear to have been mistreated. Skinny? Yes. But that might have been an inherited trait; from his size and general body type, there was more than a hint of whippet or greyhound in the dog's family tree.

"What if your real owner comes looking for you?" he asked. "If I took you home with me, what would they do? They'd be heartbroken to lose a spunky little guy like you."

The dog answered with a head tilt to the opposite side. The tip of one ear just wouldn't remain standing, while the other seemed to be scanning the background for sounds of something. Intrusion, perhaps? Additional mayhem? The return of the redheaded mugger who'd sucker punched Damian and left him googly-eyed on the pavement?

Damian stroked the dog's sleek head, a gesture the animal clearly enjoyed.

"But what if I left you here, and nobody showed up because they didn't know to look here?"

The dog yawned.

"Okay," Damian said, his voice grown serious, "I'll take you to a vet, or the pound, whichever is closer, and I'll have them check to see if you've got one of those chip things they use to identify lost pets. Fair enough?"

The dog leaned against him, and that provided all the answer he needed. He'd find a vet. "No way in hell I'm gonna take you anywhere near a dog pound. You stood guard over me. It's the least I can do for you."

A tail wag sealed the deal.

~*~

"What d'ya make of it?" asked the photographer assigned to the case. "Ever seen anything like this?"

Detective Alice Campbell exhaled heavily and looked into the expectant face of the younger officer. "I'm stumped. The body appears to have been run over by a steamroller or something, but from the looks of the ground around the car, whatever tore him up so badly did it right inside the car."

"You thinkin' an animal did it?"

"Like a bear?"

"Or a T-Rex?"

Alice shook her head. "I don't see any tooth marks. Limbs aren't torn off, but it's obvious he suffered a lot of broken bones."

She stared hard at what remained of the dead man's T-shirt. "Please tell me that's not an Alabama shirt."

"Well," said the photographer, "I could, but I'd be lyin'."

The guy from the library? No, it couldn't be. "There must be a run on 'Bama fans," she said.

"Ma'am?"

"It's nothing," she assured him. "I have another case involving a guy wearing a 'Roll Tide' shirt. But he was smaller and had... uhm... other distinguishing characteristics. This can't be the same guy. No way."

A woman from the crime scene investigation unit handed her the victim's wallet which Alice immediately searched for identification.

"*Theodore Flynt?*" She said out loud, instantly recognizing the name on the driver's license. "There is just no... damn... way!"

Turning, she took another long look at the mangled body in the car. His face was obscured by blood, and his jaw had either been dislocated or broken, possibly both. But, she decided, *it's him.*

Nothing else in his wallet suggested a next of kin, and they had yet to locate a cell phone. Alice needed his emergency contact information, then realized she already had it in the case file for the swimming pool murder. She called up the notes on her cell phone and quickly scanned through them.

The dead man had a wife, Callie Flynt. That nugget of information triggered another bit of bell-ringing. The name had come up in the craziness at the library. That may or may not have been a coincidence, but it amounted to something she had to follow up. She dialed the phone number she had for the dead man's wife, but no one answered.

Forced to dig deeper in her notes, she found another contact, this time from the library: Damian Dean, artist. He said he knew the woman who'd been the object of the crazy dwarf's search. If nothing else, he could verify the woman's last name. And with any luck, he could supply an alternate phone number.

"Worth the effort," she told herself as she dialed him up.

~*~

Callie fixed herself a sandwich while taking a break from reviewing the letters in the file from Gordon Parkhurst. Reading them hadn't taken too long, but sorting them according to the sender's distance from Atlanta proved more challenging. A computer would have helped, but she hadn't had time to buy one, much less arrange for an internet connection in Enid's mansion.

The telephone in the mansion had rung twice, but Callie opted not to answer. So many library patrons had complained to her about scams and marketers.

She had just taken a huge bite of her sandwich when her cell phone rang. A quick look told her the caller wasn't using either of the two numbers listed in her directory. The caller's identity wasn't displayed, and Callie paused before answering.

Who could have gotten her number?

"Oh, what the hell," she said and accepted the call. With her mouth still full, she managed a quick, "Hullo?"

"Calliope?" The voice sounded strained and distant.

"*Aunt Enid?*" It had to be her; no one else on Earth called her Calliope.

"Yes, dear. I'm so glad I could reach you. Gordon gave me your cell number. I'm terribly worried."

Callie chewed and swallowed as quickly as she could. *Great way to sound business-like, genius!* "I was just having a bite to–"

"I can't reach him now," Enid said. "I'm afraid something awful has happened."

Callie took a deep breath. "You mean the drowning?"

"What drowning?"

Uh-oh. "I would have contacted you if I had known how," Callie said.

"Who drowned? And where? Was it Theodore?"

"No. Theo's fine, as far as I know. This was someone else. I didn't know him or how he got in the pool, or...."

"Or what?"

"Or what killed him there." Callie gave her a quick recap of her first night in the mansion, carefully skirting any mention of Damian.

When she finished, Enid exhaled with a whoosh. "It's Spanos. I'm sure of it. Gordon told me he'd been released from prison. Now I fear he may be trying to use him to get to me."

"Why wouldn't he just come after you in Greece?"

"Because he couldn't find me. Before he went to jail I kept moving. That's why I never went home, but I got careless while he was locked up. Now that he's loose…" She sighed. "This is terrible, and it's all my fault. I've put you in harm's way, too."

"I'm confused," Callie said. "Who is Spanos?"

"He's a man about half my age. Long ago he helped me when I first found evidence that the god spices were real. Hints about them have existed for millennia, though scholars assumed they were just myths, nonsense."

"God spices? You mean the jars upstairs in the hidden room?" Callie asked, knowing the answer.

"Yes. I knew you'd eventually find them. Most of those are beneficial. The legends sometimes referred to them as the 'Givers.' Aristotle Spanos and I tracked them down on an obscure Greek island many years ago. After we'd secured them, I tried to pay him for his help. In truth, I just wanted to buy his silence. But he didn't want money; he wanted a share of the spices."

"And you gave him some?"

"Certainly not," Enid said, her voice chilly. "So the wretch tried to steal them! But he only made off with a third of the collection, more or less. Unfortunately, all of them were 'Takers.'"

"Takers?"

"Givers add to one's health, Takers detract. They're derived from the most horrid of ancient creatures. Gods and goddesses, too. He used them to disguise his other crimes. It's how he amassed his wealth."

Callie had to ask, "If he's already rich, what more does he want?"

"The Givers, and any other spices I still have. His time, however, is running out. If he doesn't get them soon, he'll die."

"Can't you just give him some? Maybe–"

"Absolutely not! The man's quite insane. That's another little bonus from the Takers. The more you use them, the more you use up your life and whatever good sense you might have had. Spanos is a monster in his own right."

"And the Givers work the opposite way?"

"For the most part, yes. Exactly how they work depends to a large extent on the person using them. I'll be happy to explain more when you pick me up at the airport."

Callie stared at the phone as if it had come alive. "You're coming home?"

"I must. Someone has to stop Spanos, and I'm the most likely candidate."

"But... But aren't you a little old to–"

"Yes, I'm old. But I'm also smart. And I haven't given in to a spice addiction like he has. I'm sure I can take care of him. I just don't want you or Gordon hurt because of me."

"When will you be arriving?"

"Soon. I'll let you know when I've worked that out. For now I want you to hide in the secret room. Take whatever you might need with you. Spanos doesn't know about the room, so you should be safe there."

"I could use the time to bone up on Greek mythology," Callie mused out loud. "I have several books about Greek gods and their creatures."

"Good. Study them. The more you know, the better. But I pray you'll never have to use them."

Though tempted to admit she already had, Callie let it go. "There's so much we need to talk about. I can't wait to see you again."

"I feel the same way, dear. Stay safe. I'm going to keep trying to reach Gordon."

Chapter Ten

"It is impossible to image the universe run by a wise, just, and omnipotent God, but it is easy to imagine it run by a board of gods." —H.L. Mencken

Damian spent a good part of the afternoon waiting for a veterinarian to examine the little white dog for some form of identification, be it a tattoo or a microchip. If either were detected, Damian would simply return the animal to his owner. Deep down, however, he hoped that wouldn't happen. The dog, he told himself, had chosen him, in which case Damian wanted to be sure the little guy was in good health.

Based on the number of people and pets waiting to see the doctor, Damian figured he'd picked either the world's best vet or the world's worst day to show up without an appointment. The little dog, however, didn't seem to mind.

Sitting patiently on the floor between Damian's knees, the dog kept an eye on everyone and everything else in the crowded room. Cats, parrots, and other dogs seemed to understand and kept their distance.

"May I pet your dog?" asked a woman sitting nearby.

"Sure," Damian said, eyeing the cat in the carrying case on the floor in front of her.

The little white dog tolerated the woman when she reached out to stroke his head but made the tiniest of growling sounds when the cat seemed perturbed by its owner's actions.

"What's his name?" she asked.

The question caught him off guard. "It's uh... I honestly don't know." He went on to explain why he'd brought the animal in.

"He looks like the dog in those TV commercials," she said. "You know, the ones for that discount store chain."

"I suppose he does, a little bit," Damian said. "But I don't see him as an icon for a discount retailer. He's got way too much heart for that. He actually tried to defend me."

"Really? From another dog?"

Damian chuckled, "I suppose you could say that. The guy was a real SOB."

When his name was eventually called, Damian carried his furry companion into an examining room and set him on a table. The dog was less than thrilled, but he calmed down when the vet came in.

With dark hair, a broad smile, and a gentle manner, the vet quickly endeared herself to the pooch. A chewy meat treat helped, and soon the little white dog's tail was wagging like a metronome.

She checked his ears for a tattoo and used a pet microchip scanner to see if he'd been chipped. Damian held his breath during the exams.

"Nope," she said. "There's nothing to identify him." She gently rubbed between the dog's ears. "Guess that means he's yours."

Damian exhaled and smiled. "Can you check him out and give him whatever shots he needs?"

"Sure," she said. "A rabies shot is required by law. So, what are you going to call him? I need to put something in his record."

"How 'bout just 'Damian's dog' for now, until I think of something suitable."

"You could always go with 'Spot.'"

"I'm thinking of something more along the lines of 'Killer' or 'Nightmare.'"

"Seriously? For this sweetie?"

He laughed. "You should've seen him standing guard over me. He might not be very big, but he's fearless."

"Just let us know when you decide, and we'll update the record."

While she administered the rabies vaccine, Damian made up his mind to introduce the dog to Callie. Between them, he felt sure they could find a name they'd both like. Besides, he had to be sure she liked dogs, or at least this one.

"C'mon, Fido. It's time you met my girlfriend. You're gonna love her house; it's gigantic. And she's got a pool, too!"

The dog gave him his usual interested-yet-puzzled head tilt.

"It's the 'girlfriend' part, right?" He scratched the dog's chin. "A guy can always hope, can't he?"

~*~

Zeus's Cookbook

Weary of reading letters from institutions interested in her aunt's collection of artifacts, Callie switched to reviewing the books she had on Greek gods. That subject, too, soon had her yawning.

The leather-covered easy chair in the secret room felt like the most comfortable place in the world, but that only contributed to her drowsiness. Still, when she heard a car pulling into the drive at the front of the house, she forced herself to stand up and go for a look.

A tiny window in the eave gave her a view of the front yard. Another window directly behind her looked out on the pool and the grounds beyond.

She recognized Damian's car right away and watched as he opened the door and got out. What she didn't recognize was the little white dog with black spots which got out right behind him and trotted alongside him toward the front door.

Which, she realized, was locked.

Crap!

She tapped furiously on the window to get his attention, but he and the dog disappeared under the front portico, and she couldn't tell if he heard her. Continuing to tap, she searched for some way to open the window, but realized it wasn't designed for that.

Eventually, Damian walked back down the front steps. Callie kept tapping on the glass and began yelling, too, but only the dog stopped and looked up at her. She watched as they began walking to one side, presumably to reach the back of the house.

If she hurried, she could race down the stairs, open the sliding panel, and catch up with him out by the pool. Though Enid had cautioned her to remain hidden, she figured it wouldn't take too much time to reach Damian.

But she stopped in mid-stride. The only way to protect Damian would be to have him join her in the secret room, at which point it would no longer be completely secret. Would Enid object? She didn't know about Damian, and Callie realized she should have said something about him during their phone call.

I'll tell her on the way home from the airport.

While she was busy ruminating, she heard more sounds from the driveway and hurried to the window to see who it might be.

She didn't recognize either car or any of the four men who got out of them. Of the four, one looked much older. Considerably overweight, with white hair and pale skin, he grasped the arm of his driver as he exited his car.

Spanos? A nerve-induced spurt of electricity coursed through her at the thought. That was followed immediately by another. *Damian's in the backyard!*

Frantic, she raced to the chair and table where she'd left her phone and punched in Damian's number. He answered on the second ring.

"Hello?"

"Damian, it's me, Callie. Listen–"

"Hey! Are you home? I've got–"

"Hush! *Now listen to me!* You're in danger. Go hide somewhere. Quickly!"

"What are you talking about? My little friend and I are walking up to the back deck. If you're inside, just open the door."

She heard someone banging on the front door, and

then a crunch sound suggesting they'd smashed their way in.

"There's no time. You've got to hide."

"Callie? Do I need to call the police?"

"Someone just broke in!"

"Where are you? I can–"

"I'm fine! Please, just go hide somewhere."

She cut the connection as she heard more noise from inside the house. Praying that Damian would do as she asked, she looked out the rear window to see if she could spot him.

By craning her neck, she could see almost straight down. Damian and the dog ambled toward the stairs leading to the pool. Damian still had a phone in his hand, and it appeared he was dialing someone. She glanced at her own phone, assuming he meant to reach her. It didn't ring.

Apparently it didn't ring for whoever he tried to call either as he shrugged and put the phone in his pocket.

Callie lifted her own phone and tried to dial 911, the emergency number. For some reason, the call wouldn't go through. She tried calling Gordon Parkhurst, but that didn't work either.

A commotion on the deck outside had her staring out the window again. Two men, one redheaded and the other bald, grabbed Damian and were dragging him into the house. The little dog was nowhere to be seen.

Desperate to do something, Callie crept down the stairs and stood behind the false parlor wall, listening intently, hoping to determine what the men were doing. She prayed Damian was neither hurt nor somehow connected to the intruders.

~*~

Spanos eased down into a parlor chair which was entirely too soft. The hot summer air combined with the short walk to the house and up the front steps left him sweaty and wheezing. The chair compressed his belly toward his chest, further hampering his air intake.

"Have you got the jammer running?" he asked his driver who had been fiddling with the device even as they approached the building.

"Yes sir, Mr. Spanos. It's working. No cell phone calls in or out, and I disabled the land line, too."

"Tell me the radius again."

"Fifty meters, more or less."

"That should do. We don't want to inconvenience any of the neighbors."

His two primary henchmen interrupted the conversation by hauling a third man into the room. "We caught this guy outside," said the bald one.

Spanos glared at the trio. "Who is he?"

"Don't know his name," said the redhead, "but I recognize him from the library. The guy you had us send in came out with him instead of the woman you wanted. Claims he knows her."

"Which explains what he's doing here," Spanos observed, looking straight at him. "So where is she?"

"I don't know exactly," Damian said, his voice unsteady. He kept looking at the redhead as if he expected to be punched at any moment. "We were talking on the phone just before Bozo and Baldy here grabbed me."

"Bozo?" snarled the redhead.

"You know, the clown. Red hair, big nose, no brain."

"Knock it off," Spanos said to him before he could deliver another punch to the defenseless man. "You can exact revenge for your wounded feelings later." He turned his attention back to Damian. "Where is this woman?"

"On the road somewhere. I imagine she'll come back here sooner or later. What do you want from her?"

"That's hardly your concern," Spanos said as the redhead balled his fists and snarled. Spanos' stomach rumbled loudly enough for everyone to hear it. He addressed the bald man. "I can't stay here; I need food. Call me when the woman returns."

The thug aimed a thumb at Damian. "What about him?"

"We might need him. Keep him tied up until you have the woman. Then you can kill him. Give some thought to where you'll hide the body so it can't be found."

"Yes sir."

"Good. Now someone help me get out of this damned chair."

~*~

Still curious about a possible connection between the recent killings and the mention of characters from Greek mythology, Detective Campbell spent even more time looking for similarities in older cases, especially the unsolved ones. There were quite a few more than she expected, though none in the past five years.

Some of the crimes crossed police jurisdictions, making it more difficult to nail down specifics. She had no intention of mentioning her theory about the ancient deities until she had more than a hunch. Being the department's "Go To" person for crimes involving whack jobs was bad enough, she had no desire to build a similar reputation *outside* the

APD.

Her diligence eventually paid off, however. She located a number of unresolved cases in which one or more witnesses described nightmarish characters. A few of these seemed drawn straight from Olympus including Pan, a half man/half goat involved in a jewelry store burglary; a minotaur-like creature described as a heavily muscled man with the head of a bull who destroyed an armored vehicle and made off with the cash inside; and Hypnos, described as an odd-looking man with wings on his back who appeared at an art auction several minutes before everyone in the room fell asleep. Three of the most valuable works on display subsequently disappeared.

In each of those cases, the name Aristotle Spanos cropped up. He was credited *and rewarded* handsomely for recovering much of the stolen property. Further inquiries revealed he had later been found guilty of fraud and the manipulation of various securities resulting in a federal court conviction and a prison sentence of fifteen years. After five, he'd been given an early release, supposedly for good behavior. She assumed he had somehow managed to buy his way out.

Besides that, it seemed his release coincided all too conveniently with the Buckhead swimming pool murder, the library assault, and the dead man in the car outside a downtown Atlanta office building. But, she wondered, what possible connection could Aristotle Spanos have had with a slum-dwelling ne'er-do-well like Theo Flynt?

The case—no, make that *cases*—had developed a great deal more intrigue than she'd originally thought possible.

~*~

Terrified by the threat to Damian she'd heard while

eavesdropping on the intruders, Callie crept back up the stairs to the hidden room and opened the cabinet to reveal Enid's spices. Translating the names on the jars from Greek to English would take some time, but she felt she had no other options. If the spices had the power to heal, they might also provide additional benefits. With any luck, she'd find one which might help her frighten off the men downstairs.

One after another she searched through her books for matches to the Greek spellings on the jars, sometimes stopping to double-check or make a note for reference later. Eventually, she found a jar bearing the Greek label:

βιάω

Shortly thereafter she found an entry describing the little known goddess Bia:

> **Bia** (βιάω) A goddess in Greek mythology, Bia is the daughter of the Titans Pallas and Styx and represented the personification of force. During the war between the Titans and the Olympians, which the Olympians eventually won, Bia and her siblings sided with Zeus. To honor her, Zeus made her one of his constant companions.

The goddess of force? And a Titan? Callie felt herself break into a smile. Maybe she would be able to ride to Damian's rescue after all.

For a long, selfish moment, she wondered what she might do to Theo if the spice provided her with a measure of Bia's power. Wouldn't he be surprised for once to find himself on the target end of a backhanded blow to *his* face?

Callie opened a can of cola and stirred in a teaspoon or so of the Bia powder. This she drank as quickly as she could, though the carbonation and the odd taste forced her to slow down.

While working on the drink, it occurred to her that Titans were considerably larger than normal people. Glancing down at the T-shirt and running shorts she'd bought on a whim, she hoped they would survive any changes she might undergo. Her only other option would be to go into battle stark naked, and while that might provide a brief distraction for her opponents, it wouldn't go terribly far in projecting Bia's legendary forcefulness. Callie decided to leave her apparel alone until she had some results from the spice to evaluate.

Drowsy, she sat back down in the overstuffed chair she had occupied while reading. Tingling from head to toe, she shut her eyes and prayed she hadn't made a colossal mistake by consuming the spice.

What if it's poisonous? That thought caused her to sit up straight.

But, she assured herself, if that were the case, Enid would surely have warned her. After a sidelong glance at a wall clock, Callie eased back into the soft chair and drifted off.

When she awoke, she was pleased to note a mere fifteen minutes had gone by. The tingling she'd experience earlier had subsided completely. She stretched, suddenly aware the overstuffed chair had become smaller, as had her clothing.

Standing, she went in search of a mirror, but had to settle for the small one she carried in her purse. Working slowly, she examined her reflection with a great and growing sense of shock. The person in the mirror could not have looked any less like Callie Flynt, mild mannered library clerk. The woman in the mirror stood a great deal taller. Her arms and legs were tanned and well-muscled.

Thanks to a significant increase in her bosom, Callie's T-shirt rose high enough to display the sort of six-pack abs normally found on Olympic athletes and body builders. A glance at the rest of her clothing proved it to be just as revealing. On the fearsome Amazonian frame she'd acquired, her running shorts looked like a bikini bottom.

The biggest shock, however, came when she examined her new face. Her blonde locks had been replaced by a tidal wave of dark curls. Her features had become sharper, more distinct. Her nose appeared larger, her cheeks more pronounced, and the dimples she'd been so secretly proud of were gone. Her formerly blue eyes now reflected a shade of green she'd only seen on photos of European race cars. Her lips and eyebrows seemed more full, too.

She lowered the mirror and flexed the muscles in her arms and legs. A feeling of immense power coursed through her along with the unswerving conviction that nothing in this world or the next could possibly stand against her. Nothing!

That included the two individuals in the rooms below who held her friend Damian against his will. More importantly, though they didn't know it yet, they held him against *hers*.

~*~

Damian's discomfort, mixed with liberal amounts of anger and fear, left him drained, his spirits at the lowest possible ebb. With his hands bound behind him, and forced to sit cross-legged on the floor, he had little hope of escape. The gag in his mouth had been secured with wire which not only held the rag in place between his teeth but cut relentlessly into the back of his neck. Bozo and Baldy had made sure he wouldn't be able to warn Callie if she showed up. Fortunately, she already knew there were intruders in the house. Surely she had called the cops.

As he ruminated on his imminent police rescue, a wall panel directly across the room from him slid silently into the adjoining wall. He had no idea such a door existed. It opened so quietly, it went unnoticed by the thugs who were watching the television.

More surprising than the secret door was the statuesque woman who stepped quietly into the room as the panel slipped back into place.

"You'd do well to leave now," she said, her voice husky and well-modulated. The stunning, dark-haired woman looked completely at ease as she addressed two adult, male hoodlums while unarmed and only partially clothed.

Her comment instantly drew the attention of the guards, and both stood to face her.

"Holy mother of God," breathed the redhead, clearly in awe of the woman. His head tilted up and down as he examined the buxom, scantily clad vision standing in front of him.

Baldy struggled to form words. "Who? Is that... Is *she* the broad we've been waitin' for?"

"She's the broad I've waited for all my life," Bozo breathed.

"Leave now, and you won't be hurt," said the woman as she stepped to one side and paused beside an antique roll top desk.

"I wouldn't think of hurting someone as hot as you," said the redhead. He moved toward her slowly, one arm extended. "So, your name's Callie?"

She squinted at him, as if by so doing she could peer inside his skull. "The door is over there," she said, sweeping her arm toward the exit. "Use it. Now."

Damian tried to warn her that Baldy was closing in on her, but the gag foiled him completely. He continued to struggle; the bindings around his chest and arms allowed little movement.

The woman actually smiled, an act so incongruous it left Damian not just puzzled but shocked.

"So be it," she said and leapt forward, her movements so swift they defied reason. She grabbed Bozo's outstretched arm and yanked it, hard. Damian heard something crack, and the redhead screamed.

The Amazon then dropped to one knee. From there she latched onto Bozo's ankle with one hand and the wrist of his damaged arm with the other.

"Don't move!" Baldy screamed at her as he pulled a gun from the waistband of his pants.

Damian could do little but pound the floor with his bound feet.

The tall, dark-haired beauty lifted Bozo off the floor as if he weighed nothing. She spun around once, building momentum, then threw the still-screaming man at Baldy, slamming both of them into the wall behind.

Clearly dazed, Baldy scrabbled around on the floor to find his gun.

Bozo, though reduced to a groaning, writhing mess, still managed to extract his own handgun and worked at chambering a round. One of his arms flailed uselessly in the attempt.

Moving with a grace that belied her size and strength, the vigilante female plucked the roll top desk from the floor and hurled it at Baldy, smashing him flat. A dark red pool of blood soon leaked out onto the hardwood. His body quivered for a moment or two then went limp.

The remaining thug's eyes went wide, and his hand trembled as he struggled to lift his arm and aim his weapon at her. That ended abruptly when she stomped his head into the floor.

Damian turned away quickly but not soon enough to avoid seeing the damage she'd done to Bozo's skull. It reminded him all too much of pumpkins crushed after Halloween.

He looked up as she moved in his direction. Though not even breathing hard, she had a look in her eye that absolutely terrified him.

~*~

Spanos had grown weary of waiting. The idiot they found wandering around Enid's estate had given him the impression Theo's wife would be back soon. Where the hell was she?

He tried to call several times, but couldn't get through and assumed the jamming device was still in use. All or nothing, he thought. Someone really needed to figure out a way around that.

On the verge of driving back to the mansion to investigate, his cell phone rang. Hoping one of his men had figured out how to contact him, he answered the call.

"What?" he barked.

"Aristotle Spanos, please. This is Detective Alice Campbell."

Fucking swell. Just what I needed. "How can I help you, detective?"

"I'm investigating a number of unsolved crimes," she said. "I could use your input."

"You understand I've just been released from custody. I doubt I know anything you'd find of value."

"Actually," she said, "I'm looking at some crimes you are familiar with, robberies. According to the case notes, you acquired some of the stolen goods and returned them."

Seriously? You want to talk about this crap now? "I was simply doing my civic duty. Any questions about my involvement in such ancient history were answered long ago."

"I'm sure that's true, but I have a few new questions which need answers. Must I remind you that you have an early release, not a pardon, and your freedom is not without obligation. If you want to stay out of prison, I suggest you cooperate."

"This just isn't a very good time," he said.

"It's funny," she said. "I hear that a lot."

"And I'm sick."

"With what?"

"Old age, mostly."

"Oh come on. You're about my age, and you know what they say: 'fifty is the new thirty.'"

"I'm a sick man," he protested.

"Oh, all right," the cop said. "I'll come to you."

"I, uh, wait–"

"Don't go anywhere. I'll be there as soon as I can."

Chapter Eleven

"We are all atheists about most of the gods that societies have ever believed in. Some of us just go one god further."
—Richard Dawkins

Callie saw the look of fear on Damian's face as she approached. Though she desperately wanted to free him from the cruel restraints Spanos' men had used on him, she realized he feared her more than them. A quick look over her shoulder at their remains confirmed it. In his shoes, she'd probably feel the same way.

She backed away, then turned and touched the switch to activate the secret door. Damian had closed his eyes, most likely in anticipation of his own demise. She doubted he saw her leave the room.

To her dismay, climbing the stairs to the hidden room required far too much energy. While she had felt indomitable when facing the two punks in the room below, her muscular arms and legs had now become a burden. She trudged up the last few steps and staggered toward the easy chair where her transformation had begun.

Sinking down into the soft leather, she relaxed and surrendered to the lure of luxury. With eyes closed and breathing steady she once again felt the tingling throughout her body which signaled still more changes to come.

Her running shorts had become uncomfortably tight, and her T-shirt had been stretched to the limit, but she was too tired to make any adjustments. She wanted only to rest and, if possible, sleep.

Later, Callie opened her eyes when she heard the rumble of a thunderstorm. The sound triggered memories of childhood walks in the rain. As she slowly regained full awareness of her surroundings, Callie tried to stretch, but her arms felt all too weary. Sitting upright required a conscious effort.

More recent memories then came flooding back. Damian. The two men downstairs. The ease with which she had killed them. She felt little remorse for them, but Damian's plight spurred her to motion.

Dragging herself upright, she stripped off the stretched and bloodstained clothes she had been wearing and replaced them with a clean blouse and shorts. Still weary, she walked back down the stairs to release Damian.

She entered the parlor and saw him lying on his side, apparently asleep. Stepping carefully over the bodies of the two dead men, she reached his side and examined the wire holding his gag in place.

Damian's eyes flew open at her touch, but he relaxed when he saw her smiling face.

"You're okay," she assured him. "I'll get you free as soon as I can."

She untwisted the wire knot at the back of his head

and gently removed his gag.

"Oh, my God, am I glad to see you," he said, working his jaw. "Have you called the police yet?"

"No," she said peering over her shoulder. "But it looks like the danger has passed."

Damian turned as much as he could to allow her to reach the rope binding him. When she eventually worried the knots loose and released his arms and legs, he rubbed them to restore circulation. "Thank you," he muttered, over and over.

"It's no problem," she said. "I'm just sorry I couldn't get here sooner."

"You won't believe what happened," he said, rapidly growing excited. "This amazing woman appeared out of nowhere." He paused. "Actually, that's not right. She opened some sort of panel in the wall right over there." He pointed to the secret door. "She just pushed it aside and walked out from behind the wall."

Callie gave him what she hoped was a look of doubt.

"Anyway," he went on, "that's what it looked like to me."

"And then?"

"Then she waltzed in and beat the crap out of those two goons. Well, no, wait. Before she lifted a finger, she gave them a chance to leave. I'm still amazed. It's like she knew she'd beat them. Wasn't a bit of doubt in her mind."

"Really," Callie said.

"And y'know, the more I think about it, the more it makes sense. I mean, this chick was big. Not big and fat, but athletically big. Tall. Way taller than me. And she had serious muscles. She could easily be an Olympic star. Or in the movies. Like a new Wonder Woman or something. She certainly had the looks. And the figure." He rolled his eyes. "Trust me, there was absolutely no doubt about her figure. All she wore was this teeny, tiny–"

"Hey!" Callie poked his shoulder. "I'm getting a little jealous. How am I supposed to compete with some super-hot comic book chic?"

"I'm sorry," he said after a quick breath and a guilty pause. "It's just– She saved my life!"

"And I'm as grateful as you are," Callie said. "But c'mon, enough is enough."

He returned her smile. "Yeah. Okay. You're right. But still, you should've seen her. She was nothing short of amazing. Simply amazing."

"I believe you," she said, "but we need to call the police." She pulled out her cell phone.

"That's not gonna work until we turn off the jammer those guys set up," Damian said. "I think it's in the kitchen. But tell me something. Why were those guys so hot to get their hands on you?"

Callie shrugged. "I can't imagine. I've never seen either of them before."

"Well, their boss sure seems to know you. He ordered them to hold me until you showed up. Some guy named Spanos. What's the deal with him?"

Aristotle Spanos. Here! That explained a lot. Callie wondered how much of what Enid told her she should share. "He's bad news, an enemy of my aunt Enid. He's been after her for years. My guess is he thinks he can get to her through me."

They walked to the kitchen, found the device, and shut it off. Almost immediately, Callie's phone signaled a missed call and a text message. Both had come from Enid. Callie read the message and looked up at Damian. "She's here!"

"Your aunt?" Damian looked around the room.

"Not *here*, here, you goofball." Callie chuckled.

"After the way that female body builder showed up, I aim to be ready for anything." He turned a serious face toward her. "Could this house be haunted?"

"Maybe," Callie said. "That would explain a lot, wouldn't it?" She checked a wall clock. "My aunt's plane lands soon. I've got to get to the airport."

"Can't she just take a cab?"

She fixed him with a glare. "You're kidding, right?"

"Might I remind you there are two dead men in the parlor? How do we explain that? Wait, I've got it. How 'bout, 'Welcome home! Watch your step; mind the bodies.'"

"We tell her the truth," Callie said. "Besides, by the time I get back, the police will be here. And then--" She stopped in mid-sentence while rethinking the idea of calling the authorities. "Let's hold off making that call until I've had a chance to talk it over with Aunt Enid."

"I'm pretty sure we're supposed to report things like home invasions and dead people as soon as possible," Damian said.

"And I'm sure you're right," Callie said. "But we have nothing to worry about since we didn't do anything wrong. You certainly didn't."

Damian raised his hands in a small gesture of surrender. "Fair enough. But you'd better get going. It'll take

Zeus's Cookbook

you at least an hour each way."

Callie shook her head. "Aunt Enid must have chartered a private plane. She's landing at a county airport. Cobb. Sure hope I can figure out where to pick her up."

"There must be signs. You'll figure it out. Meanwhile, I'd like to find my dog. He's probably still nearby, but if there's a whole bunch of commotion, like there was when that guy drowned in the pool, I'm afraid he might run away for good."

Callie recalled seeing Damian with a thin white dog when he arrived. "Have you any idea where he went?"

"No. When those guys came at me, he tried to stop them, growling and snarling to warn them off. I managed to push him away before one of them kicked him, or worse. I guess he got the idea then 'cause he took off."

"I wish I could help you look for him, but there's not enough time. I've got to go get Aunt Enid."

"No problem," said Damian. "We'll call the police when you get back. Another hour or two won't make any difference to the guys in the parlor."

"There's an umbrella by the door," Callie said. "If it hasn't started raining yet, it will pretty soon."

~*~

Spanos had long ago mastered the technique of providing vague or evasive answers to questions from anyone connected with law enforcement. He'd had a lifetime of practice. So, when faced with the queries from Detective Alice Campbell, he knew precisely how to handle them and thus manage the interview. But despite his carefully worded responses, the woman simply wouldn't give up, and the interview dragged on and on.

He checked his phone as surreptitiously as possible,

but the detective noticed.

"Hope I'm not keeping you from anything important," she said, though her voice lacked even the faintest hint of sincerity.

"It's nothing. I'm hoping for a note about someone I've been trying to reach."

"Anyone connected to the cases we've been discussing?"

"What? No. Of course not. I had nothing to do with any of the crimes you've asked me about. If anything, I've tried to help."

The detective gave him a look which dispelled any thoughts he might have had that she believed him. "We're almost through here," she said as the interview threatened to drag on even further. "What do you know about a man named Theodore Flynt?"

Spanos had trained himself to remain blasé when responding to police questions. "I don't believe I know the man."

When she asked him what he knew about the Buckhead pool murder, he again pleaded ignorance. "I hate to read the papers these days. They always contain such terrible news. And accidental drownings seem like the worst, so easily preventable."

The detective finally ended the interview. Relieved, Spanos had his remaining man walk her to the door. Convinced the cop was finally gone, he went to the cabinet where he kept his spices. After looking over the labels on the ancient ceramic containers, he chose one and put it in his pocket.

"Bring the car around," Spanos told his employee, the

man who had previously kept an eye on the Drummond estate. "You can drop me off. If necessary, I'll stay the night where I'm going."

~*~

After a pair of phone calls and some frantic driving, Callie arrived at the building where she expected to greet her aunt. A handful of people milled around, but none of them appeared to be an arriving passenger. None appeared even remotely old enough.

She's got to be in her nineties.

Callie pulled into a parking slot, rolled down her window, and waited for the elderly woman to step outside. Heavy clouds and a light wind provided some relief from the summer heat. A thunderstorm seemed inevitable.

C'mon, Aunt Enid, hurry up! I need to know what to do about this Spanos character.

She began to wonder if her aunt had actually gotten on the plane she claimed to be on. The only person still standing outside was a female in her thirties. Trim, and very well-dressed, the woman appeared to be losing her patience.

"Calliope," the woman groaned impatiently. "Where are you?"

Upon hearing her name, Callie threw open her car door and hurried toward the speaker. "Aunt Enid? Is that really you?"

The woman laughed and opened her arms wide. Callie responded in kind, and the two hugged like lost souls reunited. Both shed joyful tears.

"Where's your luggage?" Callie asked.

Enid pointed to a small, wheeled bag. "Everything I

need is in there. I don't plan to stay long. I confess, I've completely lost touch with life here in the states."

"I'm afraid I've got some bad news," Callie said, reluctant to shift away from the happy homecoming phase of Enid's arrival. "The man you told me about, Mr. Spanos, is after me. Well, after you, actually, but he thinks I'll lead him to you."

As if reacting to a siren of some sort, Enid quickly surveyed the parking area as Callie accompanied her to the car. "Were you followed?"

"I don't think so," Callie said, suddenly worried she might have led Spanos right to his prize. "But then, I was more concerned about finding you than evading him."

"We're probably all right," Enid said, relaxing. "Otherwise he'd have already attacked me."

Callie waved her into the car and put her travel bag in the back seat. Once underway, she couldn't help but ask, "How is it that you look so... fit? And young? We could be sisters!"

"It's the spice. I've dabbled with it now for years, and I've learned some things about extending the life of the effects. They've allowed me to change my appearance–"

"Dramatically!"

"–and confuse my enemies."

Callie took a sharp breath. "You have more than one?"

"Sadly, yes," Enid said. "But Aristotle Spanos is the worst of them. The others have different reasons for pursuing me. Some less noble than others. Now, what makes you think Spanos is after you?"

Callie told her about Damian coming to visit and how he'd been tied up and held captive. "I listened to them talking through the door to the secret room. That's how I know what they intended. I... I had to do something."

"You used one of the spices, didn't you?" Enid asked.

Though she felt a pang of guilt, Callie confessed. "I felt I had no choice."

"Which one did you use?"

"Bia."

Enid chuckled. "I can only imagine how your villains reacted to her."

Callie shivered. "It was violent, extremely so. She killed both of them. And she did it with such ease. It frightens me to think I commanded such power, that I could..." She stopped and gave her head a shake. "It was terrible."

"I'm not surprised. The goddess of force is not to be trifled with." She reached toward Callie and patted her on the arm. "You did well, my dear. Though you wore the guise of a goddess, you couldn't completely control her. Not yet, anyway. As for the two men, I wouldn't lose any sleep over the kind of animals who would follow such a vile man as Aristotle Spanos. They deserve no sympathy."

"I just hope the police see it the same way."

"Did they not break into your home? Did they not threaten someone inside? Those are serious breaches of the law. I haven't been in America for many years, but I'm sure citizens are still allowed to protect themselves, are they not?"

"We are," Callie said. "I'm just not sure how to explain what happened to those two. It was... messy."

"Bia's not one for subtlety," Enid said. "And I deeply appreciate the fact that you've told me all this. I have no doubt Spanos will either be waiting for me or coming to find me soon. He has spies everywhere. I imagine he already knows I'm here."

She reached into the back seat and opened a compartment on the front of the little suitcase. From it she extracted a tiny ceramic jar. Callie couldn't see the label, but she doubted she would have been able to read it anyway.

"What's that?" Callie asked. "Or should I say, who?"

"Think of it as insurance. If Spanos is indeed there, I need to be ready for him."

~*~

Damian kept telling himself that naming the dog wouldn't have made a damned bit of difference. He'd only had the mutt for a day or so; even if he had named him, the dog wouldn't have learned the connection that fast. Calling him by any name, or even a number for that matter, would amount to the same thing. In this case, futility.

For lack of anything better to call him, Damian opted for "Spot." It seemed to fit, and would have been the perfect selection for the creatively challenged, like whoever lost the dog in the first place.

"Spot!" he called.

Spot did not respond.

The thunder he'd heard in the distance seemed to be getting closer. It had definitely grown louder. Though weary of the search, Damian had no intention of giving up. Nor was he keen on venturing too far from the mansion. Callie would be returning shortly, although it seemed like it was taking too long.

"Spot!" he called again. "Here, boy!"

Maybe the dog's gay and doesn't want to be referred to

as "boy." Damian was tempted to slap himself. *You've been out here too long, son. You've tiptoed over the edge. Some muscle bound Miss Universe saves your ass from armed gunmen and suddenly you think your dog is a sexually confused adolescent.*

Then he did slap himself. "C'mon out, Spot. Or Bruce. Or whatever your name is."

Spot still did not respond. An old man named Spanos, however, did. Damian heard his voice all too clearly. "Put your hands up and turn around slowly."

Damian complied, cursing himself for not having called the cops. Fortunately, he realized, Spanos wouldn't know that. It gave him a dose of bravado. "You're screwed, y'know. The police are already on their way."

"Lovely," said Spanos, his gun hand shaky. "I can't wait to hear you explain how you murdered those two poor, unarmed men in the house."

"I didn't."

"Of course not. One of them must have dropped a desk on himself while the other crushed his own skull. I'd love to see the video."

Video?

"Where's the Flynt woman?"

"I'm not sure."

Spanos shot him in the thigh. "Think harder!"

The bullet knocked Damian to the ground, and he rolled to one side so he could put both hands on the wound. "What'd you do that for?"

"I'm impatient. And... impulsive. The next round will go in your head. Now, where's the Flynt woman?"

"They are–" Damian instantly realized he'd made a catastrophic blunder.

"*They?* There's two?" With that, the man's dynamic changed completely. The sneer on his face morphed into a savage smile. "She's got *Enid Drummond with her.* I knew it!"

Damian curled up in a ball hoping to survive the next bullet Spanos fired, but it didn't come. Instead, he heard the old man hobble back toward the house fumbling with a small, ceramic jar of some kind. He stopped when he reached the pool and awkwardly lowered himself to the cement decking.

After opening the jar, Spanos dumped the contents into his mouth and scooped up pool water to wash it down. Afterward, he made a feeble attempt to return to his feet, but gave up without success. Instead, he appeared resigned to waiting where he was for the police to stand him up and haul him to jail.

Damian removed his shirt intending to use it to staunch the wound in his leg which, oddly enough, didn't hurt nearly as much as he thought it should. On examination, he discovered Spanos had hit the cell phone in his pocket which not only deflected the bullet, but left his leg intact, albeit terribly bruised and sore as hell. The phone did not fare nearly as well. Damian extracted the loose pieces of it and dropped them on the ground as yet another crack of thunder shattered the calm.

While pondering whether or not to risk sneaking back into the house to call the police, the little white dog crept out of the bushes, terrified, and shivering from head to tail. He hunkered down near Damian's head and licked his face.

"Welcome back," Damian whispered as he put a comforting arm around the pooch. *With any luck, my friend, we may both survive.*

A light rain fell as Callie neared the mansion. The change in weather forced her to concentrate even more on the road and Atlanta's annoyingly heavy traffic. It also made it nearly impossible to watch what Enid did with the spice.

Irritated by the driving conditions, Callie asked, "Are you going to make me guess which spice it is?"

"I probably should," responded Enid. "You've certainly had enough time to study them."

"You mean over the past day or two? While learning about my new job protecting and promoting your artifact collection?"

"Well, yes. That and avoiding a run-in with Spanos in whatever guise he chooses to come calling."

"Please tell me you're joking."

"Of course I am!" Enid chuckled. "I only brought a few spices with me. The others are safely hidden back in Greece. By the way, Gordon has a letter from me which he'll only release to you upon confirmation of my death. It contains detailed instructions for finding the rest of the spices."

"They're different from those in your house?"

"A few are, yes. But you wanted to know which one I have here in my hand."

"I'm guessing Athena, goddess of war," Callie said.

"Along with wisdom, strategy, and a number of other things," Enid said. "That's a very logical choice. But wrong. That particular spice is far too demanding. It's all Taker, and unless I've prepared for it extensively, the results don't last long. Using it, however, would still be very hard on me. At my age, it could quite possibly be fatal."

"I had no idea!"

"The spices are not trivial. Their effects can be profound, as you've already discovered."

Callie couldn't have agreed more. "So, what spice will you use?"

"I'm going with Enyo."

"I think there's a singer who goes by that name," Callie said.

"You're probably thinking of Enya. Big difference. Like Athena, Enyo is also a goddess of war and a consort of Ares, Athena's male counterpart."

"Do you think Spanos will use a spice from Ares?"

"It's unlikely as it would probably kill him before the transformation was complete. I consider that one the ultimate Taker. Spanos would be a fool to use it, and he's definitely no fool."

"So, what will he use?"

"That's hard to say," Enid said as she retrieved a small thermos from her suitcase. "There are many to choose from. I'm sure he'll find something suitably nasty. I just need to be ready for him."

She opened the thermos and poured in a carefully measured portion of powder from the ceramic jar. After restoring the lid, she shook the jar to mix the contents, then opened it once again and drank it all down. "How much longer until we reach the house?"

"A few more minutes, provided traffic doesn't get any worse."

"Then you'd better slow down a bit. It will take some time–"

"I know," Callie said. "I've been through it, remember?"

Enid gave her a broad smile. "I do, indeed. So you understand that while I may not look like myself—either the real me or the younger version I'm projecting now—I'll still be directing Enyo when she emerges. I won't be able to control that persona completely as it's driven by the spice, by I'll know the difference between friend and foe. I promise you, Spanos will have his hands full no matter who he chooses to turn himself into."

The whole concept of temporary manifestations of ancient gods and goddesses had Callie's head spinning. Despite the hazards of the road, she couldn't help but continually glance at her aunt as she morphed into a deity.

Fortunately, Enid had the presence of mind to loosen her seatbelt before she lost consciousness. So when the slim young woman in the seat beside her began to grow, she would have the room she needed.

Enyo, or the version of her which evolved inside the BMW with Callie, turned out to be a formidable woman. Not as tall as Baia nor as heavily muscled, she still presented a commanding image.

Callie took an extra lap or two around the gargantuan block on which the estate was located. By the time she returned to the entrance, Enid/Enyo was wide awake.

She turned her head and focused her huge dark eyes on Callie. "I don't suppose you'd happen to have a nice, big sword handy, would you?"

Chapter Twelve

"The sound of 'gentle stillness' after all the thunder and wind have passed will be the ultimate Word from God."
—Jim Elliot

Damian picked up the still shivering dog and tucked him under his arm. He made his way toward the side of the house, hoping to get around to the front without Spanos seeing him. That didn't seem likely as the palsied old man remained beside the pool after consuming whatever he had brought with him.

The tremors Spanos suffered probably accounted for the badly aimed shot which destroyed Damian's cell phone but allowed him to stay alive. That didn't mean he intended to present himself as a target for another shot, so he used the abundant shrubbery for cover as he crept slowly closer to his goal.

When he reached a substantial gap in the bushes, he paused once again looking toward the old man by the pool. What he saw caused his jaw to drop and his sphincter to tighten into a pinhole. Spanos lay sprawled on his back, but his body had begun to swell.

Damian couldn't take his eyes off the scene by the pool. Though it took him a moment to understand what was going on, he eventually realized Spanos had somehow begun an incredibly radical transformation. The feeble, unsteady senior citizen who had tried to shoot him was in the process of turning into a dark and formidable figure.

When the transformed individual began to move, Damian restarted his dash to the side of the house. He paused to glance back when he reached the corner of the building and observed the former Spanos, now grown extremely large, as he mounted the stairs to the deck and started toward the back entrance to the house. His bearing seemed regal, and he cast a dark aura which sparked a wave of dread in Damian.

Moving quietly in hopes of avoiding attention, Damian stayed beside the house and worked his way forward until he could peer into a window which gave him a clear view of the living room where the altered version of Spanos had stopped.

Across the room from him stood Callie and a woman he didn't recognize. He assumed it was Callie's aunt Enid, but she didn't look anything like what he had expected. Rather than being an old lady, this woman appeared younger; she also stood much taller than Callie and significantly outweighed her. Like the man Spanos had turned into, she had a dark, foreboding countenance. Where he inspired dread, she radiated confidence.

Neither of them spoke, but the woman eased Callie behind her as the man stepped toward the room's oversized fireplace. He reached toward a set of cast iron fireplace tools, grabbed a poker and a shovel, then retreated.

The woman followed suit, grabbing a poker and a small, iron-handled broom before turning to face him. Damian could see her talking but couldn't hear her words.

The two strangers briefly stood still as if taking stock of each other before raising their weapons and attacking.

~*~

Callie was only too happy to comply with Enid and step behind her. Even from behind the woman looked impressive in the full-blown guise of Enyo, a goddess of war.

Moments before, when an oversized male entered the room from the opposite side of the house, Callie assumed it was Spanos, though she'd never seen him in person. Enid confirmed it and told her he had adopted the persona of Moros, god of impending doom. That explained Callie's mounting anxiety and growing sense of hopelessness.

"Don't buy into it," Enid cautioned her. "Moros has that effect on everyone, but he's not much of a fighter. He prefers to let people think they've been defeated before a battle even begins."

"I'm not the one he's facing," Callie said.

"Be grateful."

"I am," she said. "I really and truly am."

"Good. Now, get out of here." With that Enid strode forward and after staring at him for a moment, lashed out at her opponent with a vicious swing of her poker.

Callie backed away from the combat in the living room and didn't turn her back on it until she reached the expansive foyer with its marble floor, curving staircase, and grand piano. None of which mattered to her as she dashed toward the front entrance, shoved the double doors apart, and ran out into the rain.

Damian called to her from the corner of the house where he and the little white dog were partially sheltered by the overhang of the roof. She joined them, and the three huddled together while the fight inside continued.

"I'm afraid they'll kill each other," Callie said.

Damian shook his head. "I pray Spanos is the only one who goes down for good."

Callie petted the little dog which trembled as if motorized.

"I think he's afraid of the storm," Damian said. "I'd like to get him inside somewhere, but with that fighting going on…" He left the sentence unfinished.

"Have you called the police yet?" Callie asked.

"Spanos put a bullet in my phone, though he didn't mean to."

"Oh, right. He's such a caring soul."

"He was trying to shoot *me*, but he missed. Sorta. Anyway, my phone's done." He grinned. "It's shot."

Callie punched his shoulder. "We've got to do something. My phone's in the car. We should be safe there."

As they prepared to run through the rain to the car, lightning bathed their faces in stark white, and a crash of thunder sent them back to the wall. The dog squirmed free of Damian's arms, hit the ground, and raced toward the back of the house as if pursued by demons.

"Go after him," Callie said. "I'll get my phone and join you out back. Maybe under the deck. Surely there's a dry spot down there somewhere."

They raced in separate directions, and when Callie reached her car she made no effort to shelter there. Instead, she grabbed her purse and hurried after Damian and the dog.

When she reached the backyard, neither Damian nor

the dog were in sight. She called to them, though the sound of the rain made it difficult to hear anything clearly.

"Under here," shouted Damian from somewhere beneath the deck.

Holding her purse above her head, Callie ran toward the sound of his voice and found him holed up in the only spot that wasn't bathed in runoff from above.

Callie dug in her purse briefly before coming up with her phone. She dialed 911 and reported a home invasion and a life-threatening fight at the address of the Drummond estate. When asked if she was safe, she responded with, "Yes. For now, anyway. Please hurry!" Then she ended the call.

"What if they get here before Enid knocks off Spanos?" Damian asked.

"I don't know," Callie admitted, putting her phone away. "Aunt Enid told me neither of them would be able to sustain their alternate personas for long. They're both too old, and Spanos, according to her, is weak if not frail."

"Their alternate personas? I saw Spanos change, so I kinda get that, even though I have no idea how he managed it. But as I looked through the window at the woman about to do battle with him, I assumed it was your aunt."

"It was. She did a transformation just as Spanos did. It's the spices." She paused, wondering how much more to say.

"Please tell me what in hell's name is going on," Damian pleaded.

"Okay," she said, since he was already aware of the scariest parts. She then gave him a brief explanation about the spices and their miraculous properties.

"So, all I have to do is eat some of that stuff, and I'll turn into a Greek god?"

"Or goddess. There's a lot more to it than that, of course, but that's at the heart of it."

"And Spanos wants all the spices your aunt has."

Callie nodded.

They stopped talking when the combatants left the house and ventured out onto the big wooden deck overlooking the pool.

~*~

Spanos knew his persona lacked the battle skills of his opponent, but as Moros he had the ability to blunt much of her prowess by sowing doubt. His presence alone radiated fear and misgiving.

Each time she swung her pathetic excuse for a sword at him, he managed to deflect it with the shovel. His occasional counter attacks, while not as deadly as hers, were laced with psychological poison. The closer she came to him, the more effective he was in showering her with pessimism. He could see her struggle to ignore the profoundly morbid sense of death and destruction he broadcast.

Their brutal little war began in the parlor and later raged throughout the expansive living room. Furniture evolved into strategic positions and fixtures became supplementary weapons. Lamps, tables, chairs, and other objects were thrown about or used as clubs.

The number of blows landed went up as the combatants tired, and their borrowed powers began to fade. Enid's, however, seemed to be deserting her at a slightly faster rate. That knowledge spurred Spanos on. If he could maintain his physical attacks and continue radiating negative thoughts, Enid would soon be crushed.

Enid, however, continued to fight and landed several blows that would have crippled a mortal man. As Moros, however, he shared some of the attributes that made the gods superior. He felt the pain and the growing fatigue, but ignored them and allowed his anger to drive him on.

This moment—this final conflict—was his chance to be done with the woman forever, and once he controlled her spices, he would have the immortality he craved.

They fought on, moving through the foyer where he dodged the piano with which she tried to crush him against a wall.

While stabbing at each other with the pokers, they navigated around the corpses in the parlor and danced a waltz of death into the dining room. Chairs became missiles while the table served as a no-man's land in the battle between demi-gods.

When they reached the kitchen, Enid's persona seemed to wilt at an even faster rate. Spanos felt a growing weakness as well, but he knew he finally had the upper hand. As he gathered himself for one more attack, Enid dodged away and staggered through the double doors to the deck. Spanos followed her, moving as fast as his rapidly tiring body allowed.

He caught up with her near the center of the deck, and as a hard rain pelted them both, he administered a killing blow. His poker struck Enid in the back of her head. After two sluggish steps forward, she dropped her makeshift weapons and slumped to the board floor, unconscious.

Spanos dragged a chair close to her and took a seat. Their transformations would soon begin. If Enid somehow survived, he knew he could make her tell him where her spices were hidden. If not, he would be forced to search the house. Either way, he had won.

At long last, I have beaten the bitch. Olympus, behold Spanos, a new god!

~*~

The noise from the deck subsided, or so Damian thought. Rain continued to fall, and it came down hard enough to mask many sounds. He felt sure, however, that if the two pseudo-gods were still at it, he would be able to tell.

"We should go take a look," Callie said. "I've got to know if Aunt Enid is all right."

"Fair enough," he said. "But let's do it quietly, okay?"

Cradling the dog in one arm, Damian led the way with Callie close behind. Once they'd left the relative shelter of the deck, the rain soaked them both.

As they mounted the steps, a tragic view formed. The woman Damian had seen in the living room seemed to shrivel as he watched while the dark hulking figure of Moros sat nearby, waiting over her like some demonic vulture.

"Oh, my God," Callie breathed. "He's killed her."

"Let's not give up hope just yet."

At the sound of their voices, Spanos stood and faced them, still holding the fireplace poker in one dark hand. "What the hell do you want?"

Damian's knees grew weak just looking at the thing Spanos had turned himself into.

"I want to check on my aunt," Callie said.

"How sweet," he growled. "But understand, you have

no chance of surviving long enough to touch her." He brandished the poker. "Do you see the blood coming from her head? I will do the same for you."

"He's trying to win without a fight," Callie said. "Enid warned me about that. He's actually full of shit."

Spanos huffed. "If that were true, I wouldn't be standing over her dead and broken body. Some goddess of battle."

Damian set the dog on the deck and edged toward a tree branch that had blown down. He prayed it was solid enough to serve as a club.

Unaffected by whatever doubts emanated from Spanos, the dog walked directly toward him, a growl low in his throat.

Spanos raised his voice in derision. "You send a rodent to attack a god?"

The dog dropped low and snarled. His barred teeth looked sharp enough to rip open a hand, an arm, or a leg, whatever his foe dared to risk.

"Spot! Stop!" Damian yelled, but the dog ignored him.

Raising the poker high overhead, Spanos seemed delighted by the prospect of destroying something else. "So be it," he proclaimed.

As he stretched even higher to begin the killing stroke, a flash of brilliant, white light lit the night accompanied by a deafening crack of thunder. A bolt of lightning blistered the air as it streaked down and exploded on impact with the poker.

The hair on Spanos' head burst into flame while he cooked instantly from the inside out. His body stiffened then toppled sideways like a wooden statue sacrificed on an altar of fire.

The blast knocked both Damian and Callie off their feet, and when his vision cleared, Damian found the dog standing between them, still growling at the charred, smoking remains of Spanos, sprawled in front of them.

~*~

Callie rubbed her face and arms, trying to ward off the effects of the lightning. The rain helped, cooling her skin and reviving her. Sirens wailed in the distance and grew louder as they approached.

The rain seemed to have helped Enid as well. Her fingers moved in a shaky gesture undoubtedly meant to draw Callie closer. She responded, crawling on her hands and knees, before dropping flat on the deck, her face close to Enid's.

"Help is coming," Callie told her. "Just hold on. Please!"

"I'm afraid it's a little too late," Enid replied, her words coming between small gasps of breath.

Callie nodded toward the smoking remains of Spanos as the odor of his roasted flesh laced the air around them.

"The lightning," Callie said. "Was it... *Zeus?*"

Enid gave her a knowing smile, closed her eyes, and exhaled.

Callie checked for a pulse, but her aunt was gone.

~*~

Detective Alice Campbell sat at the kitchen table between the only two humans left alive in the Drummond mansion when she arrived. A small white dog sat on the floor beside them, his eyes fixed on the police officer as she recorded the usual data which preceded all investigations involving a suspicious death.

"Mrs. Flynt, I understand you were the one who called in the emergency. According to my information, you reported a home invasion and a fight between two unidentified individuals. Is that correct?"

"It is," the woman said.

"Let's start with the home invaders," Alice said. "Tell me what happened."

"Actually," said the woman's companion, whom Alice recognized from their discussion after the library fiasco, "Callie wasn't home yet. When the break-in occurred, I was the only one here."

"So, you saw them break in?"

"Not exactly. I was outside, in the back. They dragged me in and tied me up."

"Were you able to see what happened to those two men?"

Damian shook his head. "They uh... shoved me in the pantry in the kitchen. I couldn't see a thing. Couldn't hear much either, for that matter."

Alice assumed he was lying, and figured he was protecting someone. "So, what happened to the two men?"

He shrugged. "Someone beat the snot out of 'em. Can't say I'm all choked up about it. The guy with the red hair is the one who sucker-punched me at the library."

"A sucker punch isn't usually considered a capital offense," Alice said.

"Well, forgive me if I don't care. They broke in and held me prisoner. That's kidnapping, isn't it?"

"Probably."

"Well then, there's your capital crime."

Alice pursed her lips. "Okay, fine. Now tell me who acted as the judge, jury, and executioner."

"Sorry, can't help you there. I was in the–"

"The pantry. Right."

She looked at the woman. "And when did you get here?"

"Right after the fight in the parlor. Both men were already dead when I arrived."

"How did you know they were dead? Did you check them for a pulse or attempt CPR?"

"I didn't go near them," Callie said. "I didn't have to. It seemed pretty obvious they were dead. I've seen healthier looking roadkill."

Alice jotted down a few pointless notes before continuing. "All right then, let's move on to the fight between the two senior citizens on the deck. Do either of you know what that was about?"

Callie spoke first. "The man on the deck–"

"The charbroiled one?"

"Yes. That's Aristotle Spanos, an arch enemy of my Aunt Enid. She's the woman lying near him."

"Spanos killed her," Damian said. "He hit her with a fireplace poker. We could see a lot of blood coming from the back of her head."

That agreed with Alice's initial assessment, and she quickly noted his remarks.

"Then," said Callie, "when he saw us, he tried to kill

our dog."

Damian looked at her in surprise but said nothing.

"That's when he got struck by lightning," Callie went on. "It was horrible. I've never seen anything like it. He just lit up like a road flare and died."

"Any idea why he went after your dog instead of you?"

"The dog was trying to defend us," Damian said.

Alice looked directly at Cassie. "I find it interesting that the dog belongs to the two of you. Are you living together?"

"Is that relevant?" Cassie asked.

"I suppose it is," Alice replied, "seeing as how I've been trying to reach you to report the death of your husband."

The woman seemed genuinely surprised, if not terribly upset. "Theo's *dead?* How?"

"We're still trying to figure that out," Alice said. "I'll share the results of our inquiry once it's complete."

"Theo and I were separated," Callie explained. "I moved in here only recently."

"With Mr. Dean, I presume, and just in time to have someone die in your pool."

"I haven't moved in here!" Damian protested. "We're just good friends."

"Who own a dog together."

"Yeah. There's no law against that, is there?"

Alice couldn't see much future in continuing that line of inquiry and switched to another. "Did either of you go back inside the house after witnessing the deaths of the two people on the deck?"

They shook their heads in unison.

"From what I can tell, they were both quite old. I can't imagine either of them having the strength to toss furniture around. The building looks like it housed a cyclone."

"Wouldn't it make sense that the two guys in the parlor did that?" Damian asked.

"It would, and we're dusting the furniture for prints to see if they were responsible. We'll need to get yours as well. Just in case."

"Just in case, what?" Callie asked.

"In case we need to bring charges against either of you," Alice said. "We're dealing with a half dozen suspicious deaths, all of which involve you two in one way or another. While everyone else has been cannibalized, crushed, or electrocuted, you two always seem to end up whole and happy. Care to explain that?"

"I can't," Callie said.

"We're just victims of circumstance," offered Damian.

Alice shook her head, too tired and irritated to do much more. "Listen up," she said. "I don't want either of you leaving Atlanta without reporting to me first. Do I make myself clear?"

"Yes," they said.

Alice reached down to pet the dog's head. "What's this little guy's name?"

The couple looked at each other for a moment in silence before Damian piped up, "It's Cerberus."

Alice couldn't keep from laughing. "Cerberus? Like the

dog that supposedly guards Hades? The one with three heads? *That* Cerberus?"

"Yeah," said Damian. "That Cerberus."

Callie looked at him and smiled. "We really do need to get him a collar and a name tag."

~*~

Several months later-

The sale of the Drummond mansion finally went through, and Callie's new home, though much smaller, fit her upgraded lifestyle perfectly. Content to have her mail forwarded to wherever she might be, she moved into her new quarters with high hopes for seeing the world. Accordingly, she renamed the yacht she now called home *Godspeed.*

Though the ocean-worthy craft could accommodate ten guests in addition to Callie and Damian, she was content with two. Or three, she joked, if one also counted Cerberus. The boat came with an informal crew of four who maintained the boat and saw to the comfort of its passengers.

With *Godspeed* anchored in a secluded cove a short cruise away from the island of St. Thomas, Callie presided over a lunch Damian had prepared featuring tropical fare. Together they toasted continued good weather, great fortune, and wonderful friends.

Alice Campbell sipped her wine and nodded approvingly. "What do you think, Gordon?" she asked.

The attorney smiled in response. "It's the best I've had all day."

"Better than what we had with dinner the night I saved you from the trunk of that car?"

"You're never going to let me forget that, are you?" he

asked.

She kissed him on the cheek. "Not a chance."

Though each had been provided a private stateroom, Callie's newly retired passengers always woke up together in one room or the other. Alice appeared years younger, as did Gordon, and neither complained about the unusual flavor of some of their foods.

Callie had one of the staterooms converted to a studio for Damian who kept busy working on a new series of children's books which he wrote and illustrated featuring characters from Greek mythology.

Cerberus seemed content as well and could usually be found sitting beside Callie as she became gradually more proficient at piloting the 125-foot long yacht.

Near the end of the meal, Callie broached a topic she'd been mulling over for some time. "How would y'all feel about sailing to Greece? There are some things there my sweet aunt Enid left in storage for me."

Not a soul objected.

~End~

Josh Langston

Zeus's Cookbook

About the Author

Josh Langston's fiction has been published in a variety of magazines and anthologies, and both his Christmas and Western short story collections have reached the Amazon top 20 for genre fiction. His fourteen novels are split between historical fiction and contemporary fantasies.

Josh also loves to teach. His classes on novel writing, memoir, and independent publishing are filled with students eager to learn and have their work perused by a pro. His textbooks on the craft of fiction, memoir, and novel writing provide a humorous and easy-to-understand approach to the subjects while imparting valuable tips and techniques. **Naked Notes!** is the fourth title in his textbook series and was released in 2018.

Josh can be reached via his website: **www.JoshLangston.com**

~*~

Now, turn the page for an added bonus: Chapter One of **Oh, Bits!** a paranormal romance novel set in Atlanta, GA, during World War II....

Oh, Bits!

Oh, Bits!

Grumbles From the Grave

When The Dead

Just Won't Shut Up...

Bestselling Author **JOSH LANGSTON**

Oh, Bits!

Chapter 1

Perfidy, Peril, and Predilections

"You can't be serious," Angelica said. "The *mayor* did that? *Our* mayor?"

"Seems so," came the muffled reply. Digby Doolan rarely raised his voice, which made his foghorn-in-the-distance growls even harder to understand. The shocking value of Digby's revelations made the inconvenience easy to overlook. How he sounded didn't matter so long as what he offered remained juicy.

Angelica Rohrbach scratched a concluding line on her notepad. It was nearly full, just like the other eight such notebooks she kept locked in a strongbox in the root cellar, the closest thing she had to a bomb shelter in a time of war. Though it was unlikely any German or Japanese bombers would ever reach Georgia, it never hurt to take precautions. She took similar care in recording the dates and times of each notebook entry. Later, when she wrote up her column

Oh, Bits!

for the Atlanta *Clarion*, she would enhance the details and obscure their source. No one ever knew where she got her information, and she aimed to keep it that way.

"What do I owe you?" she asked.

Digby shuffled his feet and fiddled with his cap, mannerisms Angelica had learned to accept along with the cemetery caretaker's odor and his dirt-stained attire. Not that she ever let him in the house; just being in his presence provided all the nerve-jangling she could handle.

"Hun'erd?"

Angelica recognized the inflated first offer and shook her head. "Don't be silly."

"It's about the dadgum mayor," Digby grumbled. "That's worth more than usual."

"It would be if we could prove it. That a man like him would spend time with a–" She paused. "A *streetwalker*, doesn't surprise me. How's fifty dollars sound?"

"Pretty danged chintzy. The information's worth a helluva lot more. Now that I think on it, I reckon it's worth more like *two* hun'erd."

Angelica pursed her lips. "There's no doubt my readers will be delighted to learn that His Honor provided a hussy with a furnished apartment. I, for one, would like to know how he paid for it, and whether or not he used tax money. But in any case, I need proof before I can print any of it."

Digby stopped shuffling and pushed his short-brimmed cap to the back of his head. A shock of unkempt gray hair slumped forward and covered his weathered forehead. "You've started with rumor before. You kin do it again."

"I suppose," she said, trying to reconcile accepting his

opening bid with her native frugality. "Let me get my purse." She slipped away and took a grateful breath of air not tainted by the gravedigger's aroma. She found her pocketbook and dug out half of what she needed then hurriedly returned to the back door. "I'll have to go to the bank to get the rest," she said, pushing the money into his outstretched hands. "There'll be fifty more tomorrow; I promise."

"There's only fifty here now," he said. "I told ya two hun'erd."

"Now see here, Digger, we've been doing business for–"

"A long time," he said. "And if you'd like to continue doing business, you'll pay what I ask."

"But–"

"A hun'erd an' a half. Tomorrow. Bring it by at lunchtime. I'll be in the shed."

"But–"

"See ya then," he growled over his shoulder as he sauntered away. "Don't be late."

~*~

Still fuming, Digby clambered into his ancient Ford truck and nursed the rusting relic to life. As a cloud of thick exhaust fumes rolled over the Rohrbach residence, he shifted into first and eased his foot off the clutch. Had he been a younger, more impetuous man, he might have tried to spin the tires and spew gravel across Angelica's neatly raked driveway. He knew, however, that such an effort would likely have caused the engine to seize and possibly cough up one of its four dinky pistons. As crappy as the truck was, it was the only vehicle the owners of the cemetery provided for him. If he tore it up, they'd take forever to replace it.

Oh, Bits!

And in the meantime, he'd still have to haul his tools around to care for the old graves when he wasn't digging new ones. They called it landscaping. He wasn't sure what the hell it was. Grass-cutting and flower planting, sure, but the worst of it was hauling off deadfall from the acre upon acre of hardwoods that shaded the place and made digging graves so damned difficult.

Even worse, the owners were too cheap to hire additional labor. If they had more than one burial in a day, they'd give him a little extra cash to hire "independent contractors." These were usually winos and/or other down and outs who'd work for the pittance he had to offer. Granted, at fifty cents an hour, it was twice the minimum wage, but who wanted to earn it digging holes big enough and deep enough for caskets?

Thanks to Hitler, Mussolini, and the Emperor of Japan, able-bodied men were scarce, and those willing to dig graves in the summer heat of Atlanta were rarer still. Rather than pocket some of the cash for his trouble, Digby often had to pay double to avoid killing himself with the extra labor.

Years before, when still a young man, Digby entertained thoughts of getting a desk job of some kind, but he'd seen what that did to people, turned 'em into pasty-faced weaklings who spoke like they were always in church. He knew better. He'd gotten the word. Lots of words, actually. Many of which he'd shared with a local paper's gossip columnist. No, he thought. Make that a local paper's *cheapskate* gossip columnist.

He had a good mind to cut her off entirely. No more scoops, at least for a while. It'd serve her right. If she had nothing interesting to write about for a few months, maybe she'd realize how valuable his information was and actually pay him for what it was worth.

That was somewhat problematical, however, because he needed the extra cash she provided in order to pay for a few of the finer things in life which weren't possible on his caretaker's salary.

Impasse. He'd heard Angelica use the term. It meant you and somebody else were going head to head, and neither party was willing to back off. He'd avoided locking horns with her for ages on account of her being female and him being single. She'd been married once, way back, and got a house out of the deal. He'd always hoped the two of them might get along better, but it never happened. She always seemed glad to see him, but once she heard what he had to say, she grew standoffish and acted as if he had some dread disease. Measles maybe, or the clap. It pissed him off, but he always got over it. *Before.* Their meeting that day, however, hit him the wrong way, and harder than ever.

She wouldn't get away with it this time. Nope. This time he'd keep his tips to himself until she came around to the fact that she couldn't cheat him anymore.

If only he had the option of selling the information somewhere else, but the city of Atlanta, and *The Atlanta Clarion* in particular, could only support one gossip monger.

What the town really needed was a newspaper with an alternative gossip columnist.

~*~

Stormy Green sat in her 1928 Willys Whippet coupe with her forehead pressed against the steering wheel. Though the car could squeeze more miles out of a gallon of gas than most other vehicles, it couldn't do so forever. Her little two-door had wheezed its last and shuddered to a stop *almost* off the road. Close enough, she hoped, that people would think she'd just done a lousy parking job. She had one gas ration coupon left and no

Oh, Bits!

idea how to get the fuel or where to go once she had it.

She straightened, and with a puff of determined breath, fluffed the bangs covering her forehead. The time had come. No sense putting it off any longer. But then she glanced at her legs, bare from mid-thigh down, she still couldn't make herself comfortable in the outfit her former roommate, Lorraine, had sewn for her.

"It's called a romper, and it's all the rage," Lorraine said. "As slim as you are, you'll look spectacular, and not just at the beach." She handed Stormy a page ripped from a Hollywood fan magazine. It featured three starlets in matching rompers, all styled to look like sailor suits.

"They're cute," Stormy admitted. "And would be great for a long trip in a hot car. But go out in public dressed like that? I dunno."

"When did you turn into Mrs. Grundy?" Lorraine handed her a cream-colored romper with green trim. "Try this on. I made one for each of us, only yours is about five sizes smaller."

Stormy smiled at her plump friend. "You're too good to me."

The exchange had occurred three short weeks earlier, and now the cream-colored jumper was the only clean piece of clothing she owned. It couldn't be helped, she'd have to wear it for her interview.

The editorial offices of *The Atlanta Clarion* stood half way down the block. While not exactly a prestigious publication, it had a respectable circulation for a small city's second daily. Stormy hoped her credentials as the assistant editor of her college paper would be enough to wrangle a job. Though less than optimistic, based on failed attempts with five other newspapers in as many towns, Stormy tried to ignore her ridiculous outfit and focus her thoughts in a positive fashion. Failure meant going hungry, sleeping in her car, or worse–going home, hat in hand, to an avalanche of I-told-you-sos from her family. She wasn't above working any reasonable job to survive, but she'd always dreamed of becoming a journalist, and she wasn't about to give up on the idea. At least, not yet.

After a last check of her hair and make-up in the Whippet's minuscule rearview mirror, Stormy slipped out from behind the wheel, grabbed her portfolio from the passenger seat, and aimed her steps toward the future. Or what she hoped might be her future.

~*~

Angelica Rohrbach realized she'd made a mistake in bargaining with Digby for his information, but she'd become accustomed to the practice. And he never seemed to mind. It was a game, that's all. If he couldn't see it, that wasn't her problem.

At least, it hadn't been before that day. Now the old reprobate seemed determined to not only set his prices high, but to stick with them, too. It wasn't fair. How was she supposed to keep up with the vagaries of an old man's mind?

Maybe it was time for her to teach him a lesson. She had already heard everything he had to share about the mayor. Now it was up to her to find some way to confirm it. Maybe it would be best if she held off paying him another nickel until she had some solid proof about the mayor's shenanigans. On the other hand, Digby had never been wrong before. He might have gotten a detail or two confused, and sometimes the reality didn't measure up to its potential, but he never gave her bad information.

The phone rang as she ruminated on her plan to put

Oh, Bits!

Digby Doolan back in his place.

"This is Angelica," she said.

"Your column was due an hour ago, Angie. What am I supposed to do, make something up for ya?"

She found her editor's voice nearly as grating as Digby's, though for different reasons. Though Nathan Sparks ran The *Clarion* like the ringmaster of a circus, his vocal range was much higher than Digby's. It was also significantly more nasal and came accompanied by a good deal of wheezing and coughing, no doubt the product of his three-pack-a-day habit. Angelica maintained the same odor-isolating distance from both men.

"Well?" Nathan said, his voice rising an octave over the course of a single syllable.

"I'm workin' on it, but I've got some things to nail down, first."

"So, I should just leave a blank space where your words are supposed to go? Readers will love that."

"Of course not, Nate. I just need you to be a little patient."

"There's no such thing as patience in the news business. You've been around long enough to know that."

"Obviously."

"Then why do you drive me to utter distraction every week? You know what your deadline is. Why must I call you every time to remind you of it?"

"But you *don't* have to do that!"

Nathan's response was part cough and part wheeze. Angelica wondered if he was having another heart attack. "You okay?" she asked.

"Hell no, I'm not okay!" he roared back. "I've got a paper to put out, and all I have to go on your page is a furniture ad and fifteen column inches of empty space."

"Calm down, Nate. I'll come up with something. I always do."

He exhaled heavily.

"Seriously," she added. "All I need is a couple hours more."

"Oh, no problem. I'll tell the gang in the press room to sit back and relax 'cause Angie needs a couple extra hours. They'll love hearing that. It means they'll get overtime. It means my whole damned budget goes up in flames. It means everyone else on staff will wonder why they have to get their shit in on time when you don't. It means–"

"Okay, okay. I get it," she said. "Just use my back-up column. I'll keep working on the juicy new stuff I've got, and next week you'll be all smiles. I promise." She couldn't actually remember seeing him smile.

"I used your back-up column the last time you missed your deadline, remember?"

"Oh." She actually *didn't* remember, but she didn't dare tell him that. "You know I don't just make this stuff up. It takes time and effort to get to the truth."

"You're a regular Horace Greeley."

"Now you're just bein' mean."

"Angie, I swear, the only reason I put up with your crap is because it usually pans out, and sometimes I can get an actual news story from it. I don't suppose that'll happen this time."

She chuckled. "When I said 'all smiles' before, I meant it. This new story could be huge. Gigantic!"

Oh, Bits!

"I'm getting too old for this," he muttered.

"I'm serious!"

"And I don't really give a shit," he said. "Get me something in an hour. That's all the time I can spare. Your usual five hundred words of inspired innuendo will do."

He was *definitely* being mean. She'd have to make it a rumor and be careful not to identify the subject of Digby's revelation. Digby, of course, would remain anonymous as usual. No way she'd ever give up her source.

"So, you'll do it? You won't let me down?"

"I swear, Nate. You won't regret it."

He grunted. "I already regret it."

Angelica raced to hang up before he could.

~*~

Digby Doolan liked the tool shed. He thought of it as his office, even though it more closely resembled a metal-roofed barn. He had walled off a section for his personal use and installed a folding cot with a thin but useable mattress, a cupboard for his beer and snacks, and a radio so he could keep tabs on his favorite teams. College sports ruled the south, and he could usually find a game if he tried hard enough. One could be a fan without ever having been a student, and that description fit Digby perfectly.

Sports and coffins, he mused. He never seemed to run out of either.

The most valuable thing in the shed, however, was neither a tool nor a domestic convenience. That designation belonged to an ornate mirror which had been left behind by his predecessor. Digby had no idea where it had come from originally though he suspected it had been imported from Europe or some obscure part of the Orient. Way before the war. He didn't know exactly when, and if the man who trained him was aware of its history, he never bothered to share it.

Certainly, the old timer hadn't said anything positive about the mirror. Quite the contrary; he feared it and even swore it was cursed. He kept it covered with an old blanket and made Digby promise to leave it that way. That had changed over the years, but truth be told, using it scared the crap out of him, too, if not as badly now as it had the first few times.

He glanced toward it, hanging on the wall above a workbench. He kept a towel draped over it to keep the dust off. Whether that mattered to the inhabitant of the mirror he didn't know. He'd never asked. There were many questions he'd never asked.

Sometimes it was better not to know all the answers.

~*~

In a carefully hidden set of German command bunkers nestled in the wooded splendor of Bavaria, Axel Schmidt looked at the orders he'd been given for his new mission, one which had but two possible outcomes: disaster and suicide, probably both.

His thoughts were shaped in large part by the debacle known as "Operation Pastorius." In that ill-fated effort, a team of eight highly trained and well-funded saboteurs secretly entered the United States with the goal of blowing up factories, power plants, military installations and Jewish-owned businesses. Their success was intended to terrify the American population and force them to withdraw manpower and equipment from the war effort and put it to work guarding their homeland.

The plan could not have failed more miserably. Instead of spreading terror across the land, the mission whimpered to an

Oh, Bits!

end when the leader of the team turned himself in to the FBI. The other seven operatives were arrested, and all were put on trial and convicted. Two went to prison for life; the other six were executed. In Germany, they would have been shot. The Americans used their "electric chair." Axel's sphincter tightened to a pinprick at the thought.

While similar in nature to the failed Operation Pastorius, Axel's mission had a much narrower focus. The Americans were building a factory which would soon be churning out long-range bombers at an alarming rate. The massive aircraft would be flown by female pilots to bases near the war zone where they would be loaded with bombs and crewed by veteran airmen intent on laying waste to the fatherland. Axel's family had perished in Berlin, burned to ash along with countless thousands of other innocent civilians when the British and American bombers dropped their devastating loads on the unprotected populace below.

Der Führer himself had been rumored to say a few more such raids would force Germany to stop fighting. For Axel, that was unthinkable. The Americans had to pay for the misery and death they inflicted on his family, and that sentiment had propelled him to volunteer for the mission. He would have preferred to personally dole out retaliatory death and destruction, but he was enough of a realist to know that a covert operation had the capacity to do far greater damage than could one man, no matter how well armed.

The Americans had developed a high-altitude, high-speed airplane which carried a vastly bigger bomb payload than any other. The B29 could turn Germany into rubble; Axel and his crew were expected to slow down if not stop their delivery. The team would be dispatched onto American soil via U-boat as had their unfortunate predecessors. This time, however, the mission wasn't being planned by the craven leaders of the now-defunct *Abwher*. Every step of the complicated plan had been worked out by the *Schutzstaffel*, or SS, to which Axel had dedicated himself.

America *would* pay.

~*~

Stormy tried to brush some of the wrinkles from her skimpy outfit as she waited to see the *Clarion's* managing editor. A bony woman with gray hair and severe clothing had told her to wait, though she couldn't say for how long. The look she had given Stormy–or more accurately, Stormy's outfit–had screamed disapproval, though she settled for an obviously unneeded sniff. She claimed the staff had production deadlines to meet, and she couldn't be sure the managing editor, or anyone else, would have time to interview a potential trainee.

Stormy didn't even get the chance to correct the trainee reference. She was there for a real job. She'd had all the training she needed; she was ready to write.

Sitting in the empty room, she whiled away the time by filling out an employment application. She felt as if she'd gone through a hundred of the damned things since she received her college diploma, a handshake from the dean, and his mumbled good luck wish. He almost got her name right.

It was okay though; she was done with what her father called "higher education." She was on her own at last, free to pursue her dream. She never realized getting a paying job in the industry would be so hard.

"Miz Green?"

Stormy almost jumped to her feet but caught herself in time. No need to appear over-eager, though she knew the effort was hopeless. Her face always gave her away. Everyone said so.

"Mr. Sparks will see you now." The gray-haired stick figure

Oh, Bits!

smirked at her as she gestured for Stormy to follow, then turned and marched away. Stormy scrambled to catch up, chasing the real-life version of Popeye's girlfriend, Olive Oyl, down a hallway.

"He's in there," the woman said, aiming a skeletal digit toward a room that bore an atmospheric haze.

Is it safe?

"Hope you don't mind the smoke," said her gray guide. "Someday they'll pass a law about smoking in the workplace, and he'll be out of a job. Assuming he lives that long."

Stormy didn't believe Congress would go along with anything like that; aside from the fact they were focused on a world war, there was simply too much money being made in the tobacco industry. Everyone in Hollywood smoked, or so it seemed. If opinions were based solely on what the movie stars did, everyone would think smoking was glamorous. Many of her friends in college smoked, but she'd only tried it once. That was enough. She'd heard of some who'd tried marijuana, too, but she figured if she couldn't handle tobacco, she'd never handle anything stronger.

"Well, c'mon in," said a voice from within the smoky room. "I'm not gettin' any younger."

Stormy eased into the cramped, messy room, most of which was occupied by a wide wooden desk. The speaker remained hidden from view behind a handful of yellow copy paper. She recognized the stuff from her time on the staff of her college rag.

"Siddown," he said. "Be with ya in a minute."

There were two chairs in the room. Mr. Sparks filled one of them, and a stack of files filled the other.

"Uh–"

"Hang on. I'm almost done." He dropped the paper on his desk and attacked it with a blue pencil, drawing a huge "X" on one paragraph and several lines through another. He circled a word here and there, drew some arrows and added a couple symbols she'd never seen before, then tossed it in a metal tray marked "Out." In the same motion, he pressed a button on the corner of his desk which summoned a runner. The boy, a couple years younger than Stormy, dashed in, emptied the "Out" box and departed without a word.

While Stormy observed the runner, Sparks observed her.

"Just set that stuff on the floor," he said, watching intently as she followed his instructions.

When finished, she handed him her resume and the partially completed job application. "I didn't have time to answer everything."

While he perused her paperwork in silence, Stormy glanced around his workspace. A dozen black and white photos and a handful of wooden plaques adorned the walls. She didn't recognize any of the awards, though some of the people in the photos looked familiar. Among them were the governor, a state court judge, who she was reasonably sure now occupied a cell in a federal prison, and some other supposed notables.

A poster featuring the face of Franklin Roosevelt bore a quote from his 1940 re-election campaign: "I'll say it again and again and again: Your boys are not going to be sent into any foreign wars." A feathered dart protruded from the left side of the president's forehead. Numerous tiny holes in the poster testified to previous assaults.

"Stormy, huh?"

"Yes sir," she said, steeling herself for the inevitable snide comment about the notorious burlesque queen who performed

Oh, Bits!

under the name "Stormy Weather." She didn't have to wait long.

"I'm pretty sure there's a fan dancer by that name."

"I think the term 'stripper' is more accurate, but I assure you, that's where the similarity between us ends."

Sparks cleared his throat and lit up a Lucky Strike. His ashtray overflowed with snuffed out butts and burnt wooden matches. After taking his first deep drag, he smiled at her in a way that suggested a measure of respect. "So, you wanna be a reporter."

"Yes sir," she said, relieved that he hadn't said anything about a trainee position.

"We already have a trainee. You saw him a minute ago when he came in."

The room suddenly felt a great deal warmer than it had before, and the volume of cigarette smoke made her lightheaded. "Actually, I've already done some practice jobs. I'm ready for a real one."

He regarded her closely, paying significantly more time on her face and figure than on her resume. She suddenly wished she'd worn pants. And a parka.

After an uncomfortably long silence he once again focused on her paperwork. "Says here you maintained a regular column on your school paper. Got any samples?"

"You bet," she said, digging into her portfolio. She had divided it by story types: news, features and opinion. She grabbed everything in the opinion section and handed it to him.

"Nice photo," he said, holding up the clipping to compare the headshot in it with her actual, in-the-flesh, flesh. "Very nice."

"Thanks."

"We don't use headshots in our opinion pages."

"Oh." *Crap.*

"But if the folks writing for us looked as good as you I'd be tempted to change that." It appeared he wanted to say more, but once he started coughing it took him a good long while to regain his voice.

"Can I get you some water?" she asked.

"No," he said, red-faced. "I'll be okay."

He reached down beside his chair and retrieved a thermos jug from which he poured two fingers of something dark into a coffee mug. Stormy wasn't close enough to identify the fluid by smell, especially since the room reeked of cigarettes and other odors she chose not to think about.

"Which of these is your best?" he asked, holding up her columns.

"I think they're all pretty good," she said, "but the one I like the best is about problems with the nursing program. Those were–"

"This one?"

"Yes."

He handed it back to her.

"Which one do you like the least?"

She was trying to get a handle on his game, but had little confidence. "The one on women's sports, I guess."

He thumbed through them and finally held one up. "This it?"

"Yes."

He handed the rest back to her and started reading.

"I–"

Oh, Bits!

"Shhh. Gimme a sec."

Trying not to do a slow burn or squirm too much in the straight-backed chair, Stormy waited until he finished.

"Not bad," he said at last. "A little overly dramatic, maybe, but not bad."

"Thanks." She managed to avoid adding, "I think."

"So, why do you want to work for the *Clarion*? Why not a big-time paper like the *Constitution*?"

"I'd love to work for a big paper," she said, "but from what I've seen, they only want writers with years and years of experience."

"And the *Clarion* doesn't?"

"I didn't say that!"

He smiled at her. At least, she thought it *might* have been a smile.

"Tell ya what," he said, "I'll take a chance on you. Your writing isn't bad. It isn't great, either, but we can fix that. What you need is seasoning–a little time in the saddle and exposure to some real editing. Before you know it, you'll *be* one of those experienced writers, and then I'll probably have to bribe you to stay here."

"You won't regret it," Stormy said, flushed with relief. "I promise."

"I'd rather you promised something else."

She blinked at him, her suspicions as taut as a harp string. "Like what?"

"Promise you'll continue to wear short skirts. Seems like everybody who works here is a couple hundred years old. Seeing a pretty girl in nice clothes will definitely improve the atmosphere around here."

Stormy paused, her mind racing. "Uh, okay. But I confess, this is the only short outfit I own, and I probably won't get paid for–"

Sparks smiled and dashed off a note. "Give this to Audrey, she prefers 'Miz Banks' by the way, she's the woman who showed you in. It's an advance on your first paycheck."

I won't have to sleep in the car!

"Be back here at eight o'clock, sharp. I'll have an assignment for you. Screw it up, and you can return the advance before you leave in the afternoon."

"I won't screw it up," she said, forcing every bit of determination she could into her voice.

"Let's hope not," he said. "Now, skedaddle."

Publisher's note: the dog on the back cover of this book (and the front cover of *Oh, Bits!)* is a little rescue named Foster who doesn't actually think he's a dog. Should you see him, kindly allow him to remain blissfully ignorant. Thank you.

janda
books

Made in the USA
Columbia, SC
21 August 2019